EAT THE POOR

Tom Williams

First published in 2022 by Big Red
ISBN: 978-1-8383975-6-2

Dedication

To my beloved,
Tammy G,
who has spent far too much time in the Palace of Westminster
but has somehow emerged with her sanity intact.

Disclaimer

All the places in this story are real places except for the parliamentary constituency of Richmond East, which doesn't exist. It stands to reason that the MP for Richmond East, Christopher Garold, doesn't exist either. Like all the people in this story, he is entirely a creation of my warped imagination.

'Serene Selene' is also fictional, although there are real businesses that provide the same service.

The historical figures that Pole mentions meeting are, by contrast, definitely real people, though whether any had dealings with vampires is something you will have to decide for yourself.

CONTENTS

CHAPTER 1: Something in the darkness

People have always been afraid of the dark. It's a natural fear. You can never be quite sure what's out there.

Nowadays, in cities there is always some light, giving an illusion of safety. It is, though, only an illusion. The light only makes the shadows deeper. And in those shadows there is more to see than most people imagine.

There are foxes slipping silently between the houses and, rather less silently, upending dustbins in their search for scraps. In graveyards, badgers burrow below the monuments, leaving weeping angels tilted at crazy angles. Somehow navigating their way between impenetrable fences and the brick walls of suburban estates, the last of a once flourishing population of hedgehogs search out beetles and slugs. They can sense the coming of autumn and they are anxiously feeding themselves up ahead of their months of hibernation. Cats, too, are on the hunt and the tiny mouse corpses that will be presented to ungrateful humans in the morning gives a clue as to the number of rodents scooting along railway tracks, scurrying under garden sheds or busy foraging flowerbeds or overgrown lawns. In London you are, they say, never more than six feet from a rat. Exaggerated as the claim is, at night you are probably closer to a rat than you might wish to be. And hush! Can you hear, when the late-night traffic noise falls away, there is the hoot of an owl?

For all that the night is filled with creatures large and small going about their secret business, the most obvious denizens of the darkness are human. There are cleaners going home long after offices have closed or coming in to work long before they open for the day; policemen and security guards; men and women who work in what is called the night-time economy by those who do not want to enquire too closely as to what exactly the night-time economy includes; drivers of the night buses; Uber drivers. A few are rich – traders dealing with exchanges the other side of the world, wheeler-dealers whose wheeling and dealing knows no office hours. Most though are poor: the invisible toilers of the night, unacknowledged by those who live and work by day.

They walk quickly, heads down, anxious to get home. They don't notice the foxes and the badgers. If they stopped and listened, they might hear rustling in the undergrowth. There are shrubs and bushes, little patches of wilderness all over this city. Is it a shrew? A vole?

No one hears the squeak as a tiny life is snuffed out by something bigger, with larger teeth.

People should pay more attention. It's not just the mice that fall victim to killers in the night. There are those who prey on the humans too. Other humans: the muggers and the pimps, usually almost as poor as those they prey on. The rich don't have to prowl the streets to rob the poor: they can do that from their offices by daylight.

But there are some figures out there, slipping through the shadows, who are not poor and who are driven by a need for something more precious to them than money. For hundreds of years they have lived among us, hiding in plain sight. Nowadays they have ways to meet their needs without killing, but the urge to prowl at night is strong. You may not see them, but they are definitely there: lords (and ladies) of the night. They call themselves the Others. If you ever think of them, you have another name. You call them vampires.

But now there are rumours among the Others: tales of something barely glimpsed; something that moves in darkness like them; something that is not human.

The Others have never felt their mastery of the night to be challenged before, but this is something new. They do not know what it is, cannot be absolutely sure it is a real thing. But they are scared.

And if there is something out there that scares them, it should terrify you.

CHAPTER 2: Galbraith meets an old colleague

Chief Inspector John Galbraith felt older than he used to be, which shouldn't have surprised him because, obviously, he was. Perhaps he noticed it more these days because of his experiences investigating the murder of Lord Christopher Penrith. That was when he had first come in contact with the Others and there is nothing like spending time with a creature that will live hundreds of years to make you conscious of your own mortality. The whole 'not going out in daylight' thing was a nuisance, he knew, but the effective immortality that their condition conferred seemed to be quite a significant benefit.

That morning he had looked at himself in the mirror and felt more than ever conscious of his age. His hair was definitely greying and his shirt was depressingly tight. The tango classes that he had taken in the aftermath of the Penrith affair had been neglected after an initial burst of enthusiasm and he never had got round to taking out gym membership. Now Superintendent Bailey had him spending more time at his desk and less time on the streets fighting crime. The world, he felt, was trying to tell him that he was getting past it.

He put down the crime report he had been reading and looked across the office to where Sergeant Green was industriously typing away at his computer. When Galbraith had started with the police, computers had been few and far between and reports had been laboriously produced on old-school typewriters. He was, he thought, a dinosaur, increasingly out of touch with the demands of modern policing and hence, as is the way of institutional life, ready to be promoted into the higher ranks of the force.

That was Superintendent Bailey's view, anyway. Bailey was so convinced that Galbraith should be looking for promotion that had insisted that his Inspector start attending the sort of meetings that would, in Bailey's words, "give you some more experience of the joys that await you once you get your promotion." His Superintendent, Galbraith thought, tended to over-use irony as a substitute for humour.

He took another look at the Bailey's latest idea for his career development. He had found the note on his desk when he arrived. He had thought himself ahead of the rest of his shift – even the young and enthusiastic Sgt Green – but Bailey had been there even earlier, working his way through the mountain of paperwork that always littered his desk. Galbraith was to spend the next morning at a meeting of what was cheerfully referred to as the Alphabet Committee. Some Scotland Yard genius with time on his hands had come up with the title Advise, Benchmark and Co-ordinate District Efforts. "It's basically a chance to compare notes across police districts," Bailey had explained when Galbraith called into his office in a doomed attempt to duck out of the chore. "Too often we miss crimes that cross district boundaries, so now everybody gets together once a month to let each other know if there are any strange goings-on that their neighbours should be aware of. You'll be representing us on the West London group."

"We don't care what's happening in East London?"

"Hardly. Bunch of crooks down the East End." Bailey gave a snort to communicate that his remark was humorous. "No, there's a sort of super committee that coordinates all the coordinating committees somewhere in the bowels of Scotland Yard. I always think of it as Flippin' Gasbags Harrumphing Indefinitely."

'Flipping' was about as close as Bailey ever came to swearing, but his contempt for the higher echelons of Scotland Yard was no secret.

"So it's a waste of a morning."

Bailey lifted his eyes from the mound of paper. "Not necessarily. Sometimes you learn something useful. In any case, it will do you good to get to know some of the other senior officers better. After all, you can't stay here forever."

Galbraith supposed he couldn't. Even since he'd met Pole, the Other who had helped locate Lord Penrith's killer, there had been Covid, a war in Ukraine, a couple of major terrorist incidents and a general election which had returned the government with a majority so narrow that protestors had been happy to make that the pretext for a week of riots. The world moved on. Sgt Green was certainly ready to move on with it. He would be going for his Inspector's exam soon and then Galbraith would be trying to break in a new sergeant.

He'd been doing this too long, working his way through the same routines, watching the same crooks in the same courts as they were sent down yet again. He was in a rut. Perhaps it was time to bite the bullet and go for a

Superintendent's post: sit behind a desk and politic with Deputy Assistant Commissioners: a quiet life for his twilight years in the Force.

Galbraith sighed and reached for a file he had been desperately trying to ignore: Crime statistics in Earls Court. He started to make some notes. If he was going to spend the next morning at the Alphabet Committee, he might as well at least try to find something intelligent to say.

* * *

The meeting was at Hendon – the wrong side of the North Circular Road and wildly inconvenient for most of the people attending from West London police districts. Scotland Yard would have been more sensible from the point of view of travel, but Scotland Yard was the preserve of the Great and the Good and sending chief inspectors and superintendents out to the Police College at Hendon was an easy way for the Powers That Be to remind them of their place in things.

Galbraith arrived early. It had been years since he had any reason to go to the College, so he had allowed extra time to find the place. When he got there his mood had been lifted by the smell of real coffee – a definite improvement on the instant from the machine at Earls Court. There were Danish pastries set out for the early arrivals too. Galbraith thought about the image he had faced in the mirror and his promise to himself to lose some weight. Then he looked again at the pastries. As ever, he turned to Shakespeare for an answer.

"How oft the sight of means to do ill deeds makes ill deeds done!"

Fair enough. There's the means to break his resolution. Consider the resolution broken. He took a healthy bite from a Cinnamon Swirl and dabbed the sugar from his lips with the back of one finger. He began to think it might not be such a bad morning after all.

As people started to drift in, Galbraith took his pastry over towards the window, looking out on the grey October day as he chewed. There was a black van driving towards the building, the glass of its windows darkened. There seemed something almost sinister about it. He watched it drawing nearer and was about to go back to his coffee when he saw it turn sharply into a ramp that led down beneath the building. It must, he thought be somebody senior enough to have snaffled a prime parking spot: certainly no one humble enough to be mixing with the officers on the Alphabet Committee. He turned to look at the others now clustered around the last of the Danish pastries. He recognised a few of the faces but there was nobody that he knew personally. This was not the sort of meeting that would attract honest thief-takers and, for all that Bailey was convinced that it was an opportunity to network, those who had turned up seemed to be talking only to those they already knew. Galbraith did wonder about looking at the attendee list to see if there was anyone with whom he might have anything in common, but there was no attendee list. No sign-in sheets come to that. It was the way these things always are. The police are very good at explaining the importance of controlling access to offices when they do the crime prevention talks, but internal security at Hendon was terrible.

People were beginning to take their seats. The meeting was about to begin when the door opened again and a familiar figure stepped in.

At least, Galbraith thought it was familiar. It was difficult to be sure. Pole – if it was Pole – was wearing a hat, sunglasses, and a scarf. It was indoors on a relatively mild October day. Of course it was Pole.

Galbraith seemed to be the only person to have recognised him. It was not that surprising, he supposed. Pole was hardly one to make small talk at police socials.

The vampire took a seat as far from the windows as he could get and Galbraith hurried to get the seat next to him.

"I take it that was you arriving in the black van."

Pole turned his head towards Galbraith and nodded. With the scarf and the sunglasses, Galbraith had no idea of his expression.

"Section S arranged transport that met my …" he hesitated. "My needs."

"It's quite a grey day and we're in a north facing room. You could probably lose the sunglasses."

Pole took them off and, having confirmed that there was, indeed, not a great deal of natural light in the conference room, he shed the hat and scarf too.

"Sorry. I'm not quite myself – it's been a long night."

Galbraith wondered what could have been keeping the vampire so busy. He knew that Pole was not afraid of hard work, but his rather patrician style meant he avoided ever being seen to be making any excessive effort. Before he could ask, though, the meeting started.

It was, on the whole, not nearly as bad as Galbraith had feared. There were some statistical analyses that suggested the areas where there was most knife crime was shifting: good news for some in the audience, rather more worrying for others. What had been dismissed as a couple of incidents of indecent exposure near Uxbridge turned out to be echoed in several other districts. It didn't take a master detective to recognise one prolific offender working his way along the Piccadilly line. Notes were compared and the Transport Police were to be brought in. Galbraith thought that there was a fair chance the man would be caught before too long.

A couple of gangs of street robbers had relocated from one London borough to another and the officer who had dealt with them in the past would brief the new team. A confidence trickster in Hounslow had developed a nice line conning the elderly by representing himself as a gas engineer ("There's been a report of a gas leak on these premises and I have to cut off your supply") before recommending a mate who "repaired" the fault, turned the supply back on and pocketed £100 for his trouble. The superintendent from Hounslow – a weary soul in a bad suit but with an impressive red moustache that rivalled Frank Zappa – was anxious to get the word out. "It's bound to be copied elsewhere, so spread the news through Neighbourhood Watch and we'll try to get local press coverage too."

Much of the morning, though, was spent on trivia. Anything really important was already pretty well-known across the whole force, so they mainly talked about stolen bicycles, graffiti, general vandalism, and dog attacks.

Galbraith was pretty well asleep by the time they got to dog attacks, but he jerked back to alertness as he realised that Pole was sitting bolt upright (even more upright than normal) and hanging on every word.

There had been a death in Roehampton: somebody sleeping rough in the area had been found dead with wounds that suggested an animal attack. The superintendent from Lavender Hill – miles away but Galbraith wearily accepted that nowadays you couldn't expect anything as old-fashioned as a local police station – wanted to know if any other districts were reporting dog attacks. "Frankly," he said, "if we can definitely tie this to a dog, we can put it on the back burner as far as investigations go. At the moment we have it down as a possible murder and you know what a pain that is."

There was nodding around the table. Everybody there was all too aware of the cost of keeping a team on a murder hunt. If it could be shuffled off as an accidental death, or even an unlawful killing, everybody would be happy.

"You need to get in touch with the Royal Parks Operational Command Unit," said an older officer from Twickenham. His area covered Richmond, though not the great deer park there. “There have been complaints about deer being mauled. It may be that there’s a dog problem.”

“That would figure.” This time it was a superintendent from Kingston, which also bordered Richmond Park. “We had a report that somebody’s dog – an Alsatian, I think, so quite a big creature – heard what sounded like another dog in their garden and dashed out to investigate. When it failed to return, the owner went looking for it. It was dead. Quite badly mangled.”

There was subdued nodding around the table. Many of the senior officers owned dogs and Galbraith had a distinct feeling that they were more concerned about the Alsatian than the homeless man in Roehampton. In any case there was general agreement that West London police would keep an eye out for any incidents that might be put down to dangerous dogs and that it would be reasonable for Lavender Hill to stand down the murder squad.

The discussion moved on to problems with young people in stolen cars and agreement that a concerted blitz on motoring offences was overdue. Galbraith felt Pole relax back into his seat.

Half an hour later there was a break for coffee. After coffee they were to discuss minority representation across the various boroughs of West London, an important topic but one where Galbraith considered that he had little to contribute. His feeling was that given staffing levels at Earls Court he was happy to take anyone in possession of four working limbs and a warrant card and he wasn’t that concerned about all the limbs.

He helped himself to a coffee. There were no more Danish pastries but custard creams were acceptable. He looked around at the others clustered by the table. Bailey had told him to network, but surely he had little in common with these men – all solidly middle-aged middle managers whose days of honest police work were behind them. Did he look like them? Was this how Bailey saw him? Was this, in fact, the man he was becoming?

He was vaguely aware of someone pouring themselves a coffee next to him.

“Are you really interested in minority representation?”

It was Pole.

“Are you really interested in dangerous dogs?”

Pole gave a smile. Galbraith had always been impressed by Pole’s ability, when he wanted, to produce a smile that left the rest of his face completely immobile. That was the smile he was giving now.

“You noticed.”

"It's alright: I doubt anyone else did."

Pole sipped at his coffee.

"I am not exactly interested in dogs at all. But the killing in Roehampton has some intriguing elements."

It was Galbraith's turn to pretend an interest in his coffee. Pole, he knew from experience, would not be able to resist telling him about this 'intriguing' killing if he only waited.

"If you can tear yourself away from the rest of the meeting, we could find another room and I could tell you what I know about it."

Galbraith took another look at the committee members clustered in little groups. Some, he thought, were getting quite excited at the prospect of setting targets for minority group deployment in West London. The rest had presumably long ago lost the will to live. Bailey had told him to network with people he met at the committee. Surely a briefing from a chief inspector with Section S counted as networking? Most officers had never even heard of Section S, let alone had the opportunity to discover anything about the work it did. Bailey would surely agree that this was the best use of his time.

They slipped out of the conference room. Nobody noticed them go.

"One convenient thing about 21st century architecture," said Pole, "is that so many offices are designed with internal meeting rooms that have no windows."

They found an empty room and settled down. Galbraith had brought his coffee with him. Pole had not. "It seemed polite to drink it," he explained, "but one advantage of my condition is that, as I don't actually need to drink, I generally only drink things that taste appealing."

Galbraith, who had just raised his cup, took a careful sniff at the contents, and replaced it on the saucer. That, he remembered, was one of the problems of working with Pole: you tended to acquire expensive tastes.

"So why the interest in Roehampton?"

Pole pursed his lips. "It's the latest in a string of events."

"Starting with the dead deer?"

"Well, yes. But there are often dead deer. Are you familiar with Richmond Park?"

Galbraith nodded. He was not really a fan of the countryside. He preferred his parks urban, with neat lawns and tidy flowerbeds. He had been to Richmond Park a couple of times and found the open vistas and patches of woodland strangely disquieting. It was too big. He was uncomfortable with the idea of a park that you could put a small town in and still have space round the edges.

"It is, like so many parks, particularly popular with dog-walkers."

Galbraith nodded, uncertain where this was going.

"That can be a problem for the park authorities because Richmond Park is famous for its herds of deer. Deer and dogs, of course, do not really mix."

"What does all this have to do with vampires?" Galbraith saw Pole's face twitch. "Sorry, the Others."

"Nothing at all, Chief Inspector. This case has, as far as I am aware, no connection with my people. May I continue?"

Duly chastised, Galbraith leaned back and prepared to listen without interrupting.

"From time-to-time deer are killed by dogs. Occasionally there will be an outbreak, for want of a better word, when several deer are killed in a short period. This is usually traced to the behaviour of one animal which is particularly large and aggressive and which is owned by a particularly irresponsible individual. So, as was suggested in the meeting we have just escaped from, dead deer do not necessarily indicate anything out of the ordinary."

"So?"

"Recently there have been reports from some of my ..." He hesitated. "Associates."

Galbraith knew that he found it difficult to talk about these 'associates'. Pole was not embarrassed to be a vampire. He was well-regarded in his community and proud of what he had achieved for his people over the centuries. But he could hardly ignore the way that ordinary humans – Mortals, as he called them – thought of the Others. Galbraith knew that he tried to avoid discussing what he referred to as his 'condition' and admitting that Section S was largely serviced by the undead was awkward for him.

"My associates, as you know, tend to spend a lot of their time out and about in the hours of darkness and they claim that there is something unnatural centred on Richmond Park. They see a shadow, and when they look again, it has vanished." He managed a dry laugh. "This worries them as generally it is they who exist only as a shadow and who vanish before anyone is really aware of what they have seen." He paused, frowning to himself. "It's no joke though. My people are sensitive to unnatural creatures in the night. It is rather their specialist subject. Like the unfortunate Alsatian in Kingston, they sense something nearby that should not be there. Fortunately none of them have come to any harm, but it has made me take an interest in whatever is killing the Richmond Park deer."

"A dog, according to what we've just been told."

"That is what the police assume. But assumptions have a habit of proving wrong. In this case I spoke to a vet who had examined the bodies of the deer. I found his comments very interesting."

Galbraith raised his eyebrows and waited.

"Most attacks by dogs reflect the fact that *canis familiaris* is a domesticated creature. Bites tend to be to the rump and legs. Only if the prey is pulled down will the dog start to bite at the neck. Few deer are actually killed by the dogs – they are usually injured and have to be destroyed by park rangers because their wounds are too severe to treat. The recent attacks though, have shown wounds restricted to the throat and neck, as if a large dog has leapt directly towards the head to inflict a killing blow. And these animals have, indeed, been killed. They have also had a significant amount of flesh removed, presumably eaten. Tooth marks on bones are consistent with a large predator feasting itself on the corpse."

"So it's a very big dog or an escaped wild animal. I'm not even sure that it's a police matter and I certainly can't see what it has to do with Section S."

"The killing in Roehampton should make it a police matter, even if it was not murder. And if there was any, shall we say, non-human involvement, then it certainly is a matter for Section S."

"So you think that there may be Others involved."

"No, I do not." Pole's voice was cold. "If it weren't for the Others, we wouldn't even be aware that there might be a problem."

"Then what non-human involvement are you thinking of?"

"That's an excellent question. I have my own thoughts on the matter, but I'm not sure I want to share them yet. It seems, even to me, rather unlikely. I fear you would dismiss it out of hand. But, just in case, I am keeping an eye on what happened in Roehampton."

"So what do you know beyond what they told us in there?"

Pole shrugged. "Very little. Two weeks ago a body was found under one of the blocks of flats at Roehampton. There's an open bin area at the base of each block. There's often old furniture there and big cardboard boxes – all the sort of detritus the 21st century seems to attract. Anyway, a body was found with the other refuse. The wounds were similar to those on the deer."

"Who was the victim?"

"He was a local man. He had lived in one of the houses there but he had been evicted for non-payment of rent. The flats are owned by Wandsworth Council and they'd offered him a place in a hostel in Wandsworth but he didn't take it. He drifted back to Roehampton. The police would move him on. Every so often he'd be arrested and dropped off in Wandsworth, but he always ended up back in Roehampton."

"Did he have any enemies? Maybe an enemy with a large dog?"

"He was, according to the local police, a drunk who, like many drunks, could be objectionable, but generally he was no trouble. In fact, he was quite popular with some of the locals: hence his continually returning there. His name, by the way, was Paul Johnson. I realise that doesn't matter but I feel that knowing the victim's name makes the crime more important somehow. And Paul Johnson had done nothing that might justify or explain his murder."

"Maybe it was a random thing: a yob with a big dog who gets a kick out of setting it onto someone sleeping rough. It's not unknown."

"Possibly. But I'm uncomfortable with that explanation. I think the deaths of the deer and the Alsatian and this man are all connected with whatever it is that the Others sense when they are in the area. If I am right, there is something there that we do not understand: something dangerous – even more dangerous than humans. But I have no evidence other than I have presented to you and the suspicions of my colleagues of the night. My attendance at this meeting was in the hope that I might discover something new. It worked up to a point. I didn't know about the Alsatian and that may yet prove significant. There's still very little to go on though."

Galbraith took a deep breath, held it for a moment and then let it out in a sigh.

"I'm sure you are sincere, but I don't think you have any evidence at all. Unless there's a definite sighting of some animal or another person is killed, the police are probably right to file it as an unexplained death."

Pole nodded. "Well now I know the way that a regular police officer is likely to view it. It rather confirms my view that it's a little early to be sharing my wilder thoughts. After all, you may well be right. It could be nothing. But I think I'll keep an eye out for any new developments."

"Let me know if you come up with anything."

"I will." Pole's smile this time was entirely genuine. He glanced at his watch. "And by now I think my driver will be ready to take me home." He extended his hand and Galbraith took it. The vampire's grip was firm but cold and Galbraith was reminded once again of the essentially alien nature of his colleague. It was so easy to forget. It always came as a shock when some incident like this reminded him that, despite appearances, Pole was not human.

Pole left the room to find the underground garage and the black van that had brought him. Galbraith remained sitting, thinking over their conversation. Section S was powerful, with a reach that extended wherever the Others were to be found – which was, Galbraith thought wryly, pretty well everywhere that mattered. Would they really send Pole out on a wild goose chase if they didn't think there might be something in his fears?

He stretched and rose to his feet. Perhaps he should sit in on the end of the committee meeting. Diversity targets were troubling but at least it would stop him thinking about ghosties and ghoulies and things that ate deer in the night.

He slipped back into the meeting. If he concentrated on what they were talking about, he might never have to think about the Roehampton killing again.

CHAPTER 3: Galbraith and Pole take a walk

A fortnight had passed since Galbraith had been to the Alphabet Committee. Bailey had not given up his attempts to nudge Galbraith towards the superintendent role he felt his chief inspector should be graduating to. As a result, Galbraith spent much of his time reading policy papers from Scotland Yard which he felt suggested that the headquarters of the Metropolitan Police was situated in some parallel universe rather than a few miles along the Thames.

He tossed a copy of the latest offering onto Sgt Green's desk: *The Virtual Constable: integrated automated policing.*

Green glanced at it. "I'll tell you what," he said. "You read through last night's crime reports and see if you can find a pattern and I'll read your thing on how this could all be done by a robot if we only had a budget for robots."

"I think that the idea is to link CCTV to Artificial Intelligence so that the cameras can write their own reports and spare you the trouble."

"And then they'll go out and make the collar, will they? And turn up in court in a nice suit and explain to twelve honest citizens that the accused must be guilty because the computer says so? I think I can see one or two tiny problems with the idea."

"I think it's more suggesting that the cameras can identify behaviour that might be criminal and we can respond. I think the word was 'appropriately', which is tricky when we don't have anyone who isn't filling out a report, waiting in a court, hanging around A&E in the hope that a victim might want to lay a complaint or…"

Green cut him off. "You're getting old and cynical. Bailey's probably right: it's time you moved on."

"Cheeky young sod. Is there no loyalty these days?"

"Be fair, sir. If people like you don't go for promotion, I'll be a sergeant to the end of my days."

He had a point, Galbraith admitted. There was an inevitability to leaving front-line policing – like death and taxes. Galbraith shook his head, trying to shake off such thoughts. It wasn't like him to be so gloomy. The weather didn't help, he supposed. It was late afternoon, but it had been raining most of the day and the thick grey cloud made it feel that it was almost time to knock off for the day. It wasn't, of course. It was barely four o'clock, but October had that effect on him.

He sighed and stretched. Perhaps another cup of coffee would help. In his experience, police station coffee never helped anything, but he lived in hope.

He was getting to his feet when the phone rang. He glared at it. It was probably Bailey with another suggestion for his reading list.

Green looked up from his reports. "Shall I take it?"

"No, you've got real work to do." He sat back down and picked up the phone.

"Good evening, Chief Inspector."

He would have recognised that voice even if he hadn't seen Pole in Hendon.

Precise. Old-fashioned. Quite clipped.

"I wonder if you might be able to spare me a little of your time."

"I imagine you've cleared it with the Super."

"Of course."

"I'll see you in half an hour."

He tossed his copy of *The Virtual Constable* into a drawer and headed for the door.

* * *

Chief Inspector Pole's flat had not changed since Galbraith had last been there.

He supposed that after a few hundred years you have everything arranged the way you like it, so why alter anything?

Pole poured a malt without asking. In the years since he had last drunk with Pole, Galbraith had taken to enjoying whisky, experimenting with the products of a range of distilleries. He didn't recognise this one, but he knew enough by now to acknowledge it as something rather special. Beyond his price range, he suspected.

Pole allowed him to enjoy his drink undisturbed, watching him with a half-smile on his face.

Galbraith put the glass down and nodded approvingly.

"It's very good, but I imagine you've not got me here for a tasting session. Does this mean there's news about the Roehampton death?"

"In a manner of speaking, yes. There's been another death."

Galbraith raised an eyebrow but said nothing. He had learned early on in his career that the best way to get people to tell you things is to stay quiet and let them speak. If this meant some people thought he was a bit plodding and dull, it was a mistake that they realised around the time that he read his interview notes back to them with the interesting bits highlighted.

After a short pause, Pole, barely showing his disappointment with Galbraith's lack of response, went on. "This one was rather nearer home than Roehampton."

"Nearer to home?"

"Geographically, yes. It was on the World's End Estate, just the other end of the King's Road."

"Handy for Brompton Cemetery." Galbraith had spoken without thinking and almost immediately regretted it.

Pole's face was expressionless, but Galbraith thought there was an edge to his voice as he replied. "But there is no evidence that anyone from the cemetery was involved. As I say, there is nothing to link any of this with the Others."

"But you are linking it with the Roehampton killing."

"There are similarities. Wounds consistent with attack by a large animal, body found in a bin area by a block of flats. After the meeting of the committee to Advise, Benchmark and Co-ordinate District Efforts" (Galbraith was amused that Pole used its full name) "even your colleagues covering World's End have suggested that there could be a problem with dogs. Not that they appear to be planning on doing anything about it. I think they rather like the idea. It's so much more convenient to file it away as an animal attack rather than to have it adding to the murder statistics."

"So you think it's murder?"

"In a manner of speaking."

Galbraith leaned forward, raising an admonitory finger. "Either it is or it isn't. We're not lawyers, Pole. I'm not concerned with questions of manslaughter or diminished responsibility. Do you think he was the victim of a dog attack or do you think someone killed him? Including killing him by setting a dog onto him."

"Another whisky?" It wasn't really a question: Pole was pouring it as he spoke. He waited until Galbraith had raised his glass before he continued.

"I think I mentioned at our last meeting that I was concerned that there might be something unnatural involved in these killings."

"You said that some of the Others had that feeling. You were noticeably reluctant to share your thoughts on what it might be."

"Just so. I'm flattered that you remembered."

Galbraith grunted. Pole's attempts to butter him up were out of character. It suggested that something was seriously worrying him.

"I think I might have an idea."

Galbraith waited. As ever with Pole, he would tell his story eventually if left to get on with it.

The silence stretched on longer than Galbraith expected. Pole had sat back in his seat, hands clasped together, apparently struggling to think how to proceed.

Abruptly he got to his feet and, walking to the windows, pulled aside one of the curtains that were kept permanently drawn and peered out.

"Look, it's almost dark. Give me a few minutes to get ready and I'd like to show you something." He didn't wait for Galbraith to reply but vanished into the back of his apartment where, presumably, the bedrooms were. Galbraith found himself wondering about the practicalities of vampire life. Did the Others sleep during the day, like regular people did at night? Or did they lie stretched out in coffins like the vampires in horror movies? Did they dream? Did they wake from sleep, as Galbraith found that he did increasingly often as he grew older? And, if so, did they wander around their shaded apartments like ghosts haunting their own homes? Or did they just read a couple of chapters of a good book until they were ready to sleep again, as he did himself? These were not questions he could ever imagine putting to Pole, but they preyed on his mind sometimes when he thought of the man (could he even call him a man?) he had come to consider a friend.

Pole emerged a few minutes later with his trademark sunglasses, scarf, and hat. He was wearing leather gloves and only a tiny bit of the skin around his nose and a narrow band below this hat was exposed. That glistened in a way that suggested the enthusiastic application of sunscreen.

Galbraith twitched the curtain aside. The streetlamps were already on.

"Do you think that's all really necessary?"

Pole sniffed. "If you have my condition, you don't get to live for several centuries by taking unnecessary risks."

He crossed to the door, Galbraith trailing after him. He knew without being told that they were off for another of Pole's route marches across London. For all that the vampire talked of not taking risks, he did like wandering around London on foot. Perhaps it was some sort of folk memory: stalking the city by night. Whatever the reason, Galbraith wished that he would sometimes take an Uber and spare their legs.

Pole set off along the King's Road with his usual enthusiastic stride. Galbraith did not approve. Policemen, he thought, should perambulate slowly and magisterially. As it was, Pole's pace left Galbraith with little breath for talking, not normally a problem as Pole was usually happy to keep up a running commentary on their progress. Not tonight, though. He strode on with hardly a word. Something was definitely worrying him.

Pole didn't slow until they arrived at the World's End estate, where he turned sharply off from the main road and into the pedestrian concourse in front of the council flats.

Between the flats and the King's Road is a little row of shops and Pole led the way into a service yard behind them.

Tattered police cordon tape fluttered from railings. The noise from the traffic was muted by the row of shops. Behind them a multi-storey car park and blocks of flats cut off the light, the gloom accentuated rather than relieved by the occasional illuminated window.

Behind the shops there was a railed-off bin area. The railings were about seven feet high and the gate was locked. "It's for commercial waste. They don't want anybody else able to dump their rubbish in it."

Galbraith looked: a low brick wall and railings above. It was a common enough arrangement.

"So?"

"That's where the body was found."

Galbraith went and rattled at the gate. It was definitely locked. "Perhaps it was open last night."

"Not according to the constable who was first on the scene. But, in any case…" Pole hesitated. "I think you should see the photos forensics took. I have bigger ones in my flat, but these should give you an idea."

He drew some postcard-size pictures from his jacket pocket and passed them to Galbraith, who moved out of the service yard and towards the road where there was more light from the streetlamps. He had never seen anyone carry reduced size copies of crime-scene photographs before, but it seemed quite natural for Pole. He would not carry anything that might disturb the hang of his suit.

When he could see the pictures properly, he rather wished that he could not. There was an awful lot of blood. The victim's throat seemed to have been torn out and there were bite marks moving down towards the chest. Galbraith peered at them.

"Definitely an animal. I'm no expert but I'd still go for big dog."

"Hmmm."

Galbraith remembered how much Pole's 'Hmmms' annoyed him.

"The important thing," Pole said, "isn't the wounds, but where we find the body."

Galbraith looked at the photo again. The corpse was sprawled across the top of the dumpster.

"Ah!"

"Precisely," said Pole. "I'd say it's pretty clear that the body was thrown there. And, even in the unlikely event that the gate was unlocked, what dog is going to throw its prey onto something that stands several feet off the ground?"

"Perhaps it was dragged there?"

"Hardly. There are no blood smears, no wounds consistent with something pulling at the body – and the corpse looks much more as if it had been thrown there than dragged. Just look at the way it's lying with the limbs dangling at all angles."

"So a man with a dog. Dog kills victim – who was the victim anyway?"

"Oliver Sperling, known as Ollie. Of no fixed abode or, more straightforwardly, a street person. Known to the local police. Did the odd bit of dealing to support his own habit – and before you ask, never enough for somebody to feel the need for an elaborate killing to 'send a message'. Much the same as at Roehampton. No apparent motive."

"So we have a man who enjoys killing vagrants with a big dog. Once the victim is dead, he opens the gate – you can't prove it was locked at the time of the crime – and leaves the body on top of dumpster."

"Have you ever had any reason to conceal a body?"

Galbraith shook his head. It was not the sort of situation he had ever found himself in, but he had an unpleasant suspicion that Pole might have first-hand knowledge of the mechanics of dealing with corpses.

"Take it from me, they're heavy. You might find the gate open and drag the body into the enclosure but then you'd leave it on the ground, tucked away in the shadows. No normal person is going to lift it and throw it like that."

"No normal person. But..." He jerked his head in the direction of Brompton Cemetery.

Pole gave him a weary look.

"You've been watching too many horror movies again. Yes, the Others possess physical advantages, mainly because we have had centuries to train and perfect our skills. But we are not cinematic super-heroes, capable of extraordinary feats of strength. And in any case, what benefit do the Others gain from this?"

"There is quite a lot of blood."

"There is indeed. And you have seen bodies that have been killed to feed. And that's the point. We feed on blood. The corpses of those killed by the Others are remarkable for the *absence* of blood. And these bodies have been violated by somebody – or something – that has devoured the flesh. None of my kind would ever do such a thing. We would recoil from the idea even more than you would. No, I think that something even older than my race is at the root of this."

Pole fell silent. Galbraith was sure that he was waiting to be asked and for a while he felt that he would not give the Section S detective that satisfaction. In the end, though, he gave in.

"So what do you think was responsible?"

Pole gave a tight smile. "Really, Chief Inspector, would you have me hazard a guess? You are always such a champion of proper police procedure. Shouldn't we be knocking on doors and trying to find witnesses?"

Galbraith looked round the yard. It was a strictly utilitarian space and the few windows he could see were high above. The architect had, reasonably enough, thought there was no point in giving people a view of the place.

"I doubt anyone would have seen anything."

"I was rather wondering if they might have heard anything."

Galbraith raised an eyebrow. "And you think that two chief inspectors should spend their evening door-knocking in the hope that someone might have heard something? Like a dog barking maybe?"

"Indulge me, Chief Inspector."

Why not? thought Galbraith. If he asked for a couple of constables to do the door-to-door outside his own manor there would be a mass of paperwork and he'd still have to spend time briefing them. Might as well do the job himself.

"I'll take the low-rise; you can start on the tower."

Pole nodded and strode off towards the entrance to the tower block. In the dimness of the service yard his tall, angular figure was exactly what a vampire was supposed to look like. Galbraith hoped he didn't startle any of the residents. He shrugged. Pole had been a policeman much longer than he had: presumably he knew his business. He started off around the low-rise block, trying to find the entrance.

It had been a while since he had done a house-to-house. He had almost forgotten the doors not answered – no-one admitting to being home to the police, even when he could hear the TV blaring away inside. There were suspicious looks and hostile looks and quite a few guilty looks that, on another day, he might have been interested in following up.

And amidst all the hostility, there were two people who had, indeed, heard a dog.

He and Pole had agreed to give it half an hour. They met back by the dumpster.

"So there was a dog," said Galbraith. "Proving what, exactly?"

"That rather depends," said Pole. "Did they say it barked?"

Now he came to think of it, they hadn't.

"Because," Pole added, "the gentleman I spoke to said they heard it howl."

Galbraith thought about what he had been told. "An animal cry, like a dog." Not a bark: a cry.

"Does it matter?"

"I rather think it might." Pole turned towards the dumpster and sniffed. Galbraith automatically sniffed too and then rather wished he hadn't.

"This isn't the most salubrious of places to chat. Why not return to my apartment?" He smiled reassuringly. "I have food." Galbraith remembered the last time he had eaten with Pole and the rather eclectic mix of ingredients that had made up the meal. Vampires, he knew, had learned to enjoy fine food as much as anybody but, not actually needing to eat, it never occurred to them that a selection of caviars and foie gras did not constitute a meal.

Pole must have noticed Galbraith's hesitation.

"I bought eggs. I do a rather nice omelette, or crêpes Suzette." He paused, observing Galbraith's face. "Or …" He seemed to be taking a breath, as if bracing himself for what he had to say. "There's always takeaway."

Galbraith grinned. "I don't think we need go that far."

Pole let out a sigh of relief and started back towards the King's Road.

Galbraith fell in beside him. The walk, he supposed, would do him good.

* * *

An hour later Galbraith was back in what he was coming to think of as 'his' armchair in Pole's flat. The vampire, it turned out, could make an excellent omelette when he put his mind to it. It was light and fluffy and filled with mushrooms which had been fried in olive oil with a liberal helping of garlic. Galbraith felt that the garlic was there to make a point.

They had avoided any talk about the case while they ate. Pole had asked Galbraith how his tango was progressing (Galbraith rather wondered how he knew he had taken it up) and they had chatted a bit about police station gossip, though Pole, who never seemed to see the inside of a station, had little to contribute. Galbraith found himself struggling to find any conversational openers with his host. Polite enquiries about conditions in the cemetery were likely to go down rather badly and he couldn't think of any other obvious talking points. Instead he confined himself to praising Pole's cooking.

"How did you learn to cook like that? Omelettes should be easy, but mine always come out a bit leathery."

"The trick is a very clean pan, a high heat and a little water added to the mix. The steam is what keeps it so light. Mr Soyer explained it all to me when he was at the Reform Club."

"You're in the Reform Club?"

"Oh, not nowadays. It's become quite vulgar now. No, I joined mainly for the library. There weren't many libraries as good as that that one could readily access in the 1850s. The British Library was all very well but they let in fellows like that Herr Marx. I rather preferred the Reform Club and Soyer really was an excellent cook."

Galbraith's idea of a club stopped short at the working men's club that his father had drunk at when he was a child. He had let Pole choose the conversational direction after that.

Now, as they relaxed with the inevitable whisky, Pole returns to the subject of libraries. “Nowadays, of course, one can find so much on the Internet, but I can't help feeling that nothing beats a good selection of books.”

He rose from his chair and stepped over to a bookcase that covered much of one wall. Galbraith, who associated bookcases with the splash of colour that book jackets could give to a room, had hardly noticed this one with its shelves of leather-bound volumes.

Pole reached for a book that stood at the end of the third shelf up. The title was embossed in gold on the spine: *De La Démonomanie des Sorciers*. “This was published in 1580. It was very influential at the time.”

Pole moved a small table next to the armchair. He set the book down on it and opened it carefully. “It was written by a man called Jean Bodin and it is the first book we know of to discuss werewolves.”

“Really.”

Pole looked up from the book and fixed a stern eye on Galbraith. “You are a loss to the stage, Chief Inspector. The amount of contempt you put into one word would wither a medium-sized theatre.”

He went back to his book, turning the pages carefully. “Your scepticism, it must be said, was shared by many of the writers who followed Bodin. They argued that men are made in God’s image and that they cannot change into other creatures. God would not allow that power to Satan. People have, indeed, confessed to being werewolves, but they are deluded. They might be bewitched to believe they are werewolves. They might even howl and claw at their enemies, but they remain, physically, men.”

“That seems reasonable enough. Why doesn’t this Bodin agree?” Galbraith leaned over to look at the book but the dense print was in French and he doubted that his O-level language was up to reading it.

Pole had found the page he was after and his eyes skimmed over it as he spoke. “Bodin quotes witnesses. Here, for example: he cites a court case from 1573 about one Gilles Garnier from Lyon *en forme de loup garou* – that’s a sort of wolf (*un loup*) which we would usually call a werewolf. Anyway, this gentleman attacked a young girl, killed her, and started to eat her. He later went on to attack others and, when finally caught, confessed, and was burned alive.” Pole turned a page. “There are others too. There was a Pierre Burgot who was accused alongside a Michel Verdun of worshipping the devil who allowed them to take the form of wolves and later turned them back into men.”

"And you believe that?"

"Until tonight I wasn't sure. I find it useful to keep an open mind in my line of work."

"And does Monsieur Bodin give any reason why men should change into wolves?"

"Oddly enough, he does. For men are changed by the power of Satan and they are changed to the animal that reflects their evil nature. Hence wolves."

Galbraith had watched his share of nature documentaries. "That seems a little unfair on wolves."

Pole closed the book. "I rather agree. What is being described isn't a wolf. In fact, it's not even called a wolf. I've just mentioned that the French call them *loup garous* or in Picardy *loup varous*. The Greeks call them *Lycanthropes* while you are probably most familiar with the German name: *Wer Wölf*. So let us go with 'were-wolves'."

Galbraith nodded. He was a firm believer in the idea that if you had nothing to say, it was probably best to say nothing.

"Back in the 16th century were-wolves were mainly seen as something that came from Africa or Asia. Bodin talks about there being 150 seen in Constantinople in 1542. The Sultan drove them out of the city in front of large numbers of witnesses. They weren't really an issue in Western Europe – hence, presumably, the scepticism about Bodin's account. But there have been reports over the past few hundred years. They've been vague. Unsubstantiated. But they keep coming up. I've watched out for them."

"Why the interest?"

"Don't be naïve, Chief Inspector. Section S deals with things outside the normal run of crime. You and I know that our principal concern is events that might involve the Others, but we get caught up in all sorts of other things. And we need to stay on top of them. Even you saw an unexplained killing near Brompton Cemetery and decided that the Others might be involved."

Galbraith had the decency to look embarrassed.

"And, in any event, this could be a fascinating case. If it is a werewolf – and I'm increasingly suspicious that it is – it will be the first proven werewolf incident in this country. Doesn't that generate even a frisson of excitement?"

"It generates a horrible feeling that we are going to find ourselves rapidly out of our depth."

Pole smiled. "If you were relying on the men and women in blue, I'm sure you're right, but we have friends on our side. The werewolf prowls the streets for prey at night. Who else might fit that description, hmmm?"

For once, Galbraith thought that 'hmmm' summed up exactly how he felt.

CHAPTER 4: The Member of Parliament for East Richmond

A couple of years ago, one of the Sunday supplements had done a feature on Christopher Garold. It was generally very positive. Most of the articles written about him were positive, especially those written by women. He had a certain charm which he used quite blatantly when he wanted favourable press coverage. The odd thing was, and it bewildered him as much as anybody else, that however blatant the flattery, it always seemed to work. The article had said that he had enjoyed a privileged upbringing that had provided an untroubled childhood.

He knew that the journalist had not intended any harm. In fact, by the end of the interview the two of them had been flirting so outrageously that he had seriously considered arranging to meet her again when her tape recorder was firmly switched off. The article had annoyed him, though. Partly because, in these egalitarian times the suggestion of privilege always had the potential to damage him politically, but also because he was quite certain that it was not true. His childhood had been far from untroubled.

Admittedly his father had been what he and his friends would call "comfortably off" (only common people say "rich") but when he was young his grandfather was still alive. His grandfather's childhood could not be called privileged in any sense of the word. He had been born in Istanbul and had come to London as a refugee. Back in those days there hadn't been such a sharp distinction between 'refugee' and 'economic migrant'. Christopher Garold occasionally allowed himself to wonder if his grandfather would even be allowed in the country these days, but he took care not to wonder too long or aloud.

The reason that grandfather had left Turkey was never talked about. It certainly hadn't been simply to build a better life in Britain. There had, young Christopher realised, been some sort of scandal, but exactly what sort of scandal had never been clear.

Grandfather was always referred to in the family as Dede – though that was one of the few Turkish words Christopher ever heard at home. Dede had arrived in England with almost nothing, but he had been an astute businessman and had built up a respectable fortune. He was always conscious, though, of never quite belonging. It was this desire to "belong" and be accepted by the people of his adopted country that had driven him to buy a grand house near West London's Richmond Park. With a dozen bedrooms and outbuildings for housing staff, it was a ridiculous establishment for Dede (his wife was long since dead), his son and daughter-in-law and, in time, young Christopher. It didn't quite work either. The people he was so anxious to impress came to the house and ate the dinners his chef cooked and sampled the wines from his extensive cellar, but behind their hands they muttered about vulgarity and foreigners and other words that nowadays could not be repeated in polite society.

Dede realised, eventually, that he would never be, as some of his neighbours in those days said, "quite the thing." He was determined, though, that his son would be accepted as a "proper Englishman." (Christopher remembered his grandfather using just that phrase when he was a small boy and, even then, how embarrassing he thought it.) His son duly obliged, becoming the MP for the area.

Christopher was twelve at the time, just entering puberty. It was a difficult period, especially as his mother had died, struck down by cancer when Christopher was only eight years old. Early teens are difficult for most boys and having no mother and with his father starting out in public life, it was bound to be particularly difficult for young Christopher. But in his case there was another issue that made life even harder.

He began to change.

Fair enough: all boys his age begin to change. They grow suddenly taller and begin sprouting hair in unexpected places. For most boys, though, these changes do not happen overnight. And the increase in height is not accompanied by the sudden development of a long muzzle and over-developed canine teeth. Nor does the sprouting hair cover the whole of their bodies.

Christopher also found that he was suddenly driven by new appetites: not the interest in young women that was gripping his schoolmates, but a frantic desire for raw meat.

His grandfather was old now, confined to a wheelchair, but he remained sharp as a tack, overseeing his son's career and the family's fortune. Now he summoned Christopher to his bedroom (he did most of his business from his bedroom by then) and tried to provide some reassurance. It was nothing to be alarmed about, he explained. It ran in the family.

"My father..." Young Christopher could hardly believe it. Why had nobody told him?

Yes, his father too. And nobody had told him because it was a secret. And they hadn't known – not absolutely known – that it would happen to him. But it was nothing to be worried about. The changes would reverse every morning, exactly as they had so far. It was only a few days every month. Nobody need know.

What about the hunger? Well, Dede explained, one reason for buying this house was its proximity to Richmond Park and the herds of deer that wandered there. The park was empty at night and the deer were almost tame. It would be easy to feed in the darkness and slip back home with no-one any the wiser.

So Christopher Garold's life had changed. He had enjoyed the park as a child, walking there with Dede or with his parents. He had lost interest in the place when his mother died, dealing with his grief by throwing himself into games with his friends. The changes in his life, though, were making a boundary between himself and his schoolmates. He was, he felt, special: better than them.

As he drew away from other children, so he found himself drawn towards the park and the animals. An interest in the deer was natural enough, given that they were the means to satisfy his new-found appetites, but he found himself fascinated by all the animals that haunted the place. There were badgers and foxes as well as smaller creatures: the rabbits and the hedgehogs, not to mention the little things that scurried in the grass like the rats, voles and mice. Then there were so many birds. At night he would catch a glimpse of owls drifting silently through the trees or soaring over the open grass, almost lost in the darkness. By day there were skylarks, woodpeckers, kestrels, and a host of others.

As he spent more time in the park, he began to photograph the animals and birds there. It turned out he had a talent for this. He would sit motionless for hours, waiting for the right shot. He could move noiselessly through the woodland to find a woodpecker feeding its young in a hollowed-out tree trunk, or glide along a riverbank to where a kingfisher waited for its prey. Oddly enough, the only creatures he could not get close to were the deer. Even in his human form there was something about him that panicked them. He had no idea what they reacted to. His scent, maybe? Nobody had ever remarked that there was anything unusual about the smell of him, though he applied generous amounts of body spray just to be sure.

He submitted one or two of his better pictures to a photographic competition and won. Encouraged, he bought a new camera with a longer lens and began to learn how to get professional standard results. As his photos started to appear regularly in magazines, it seemed natural for him to write about the animals in his pictures and he started to get a reputation as someone who cared about the natural world.

His father was getting older and Christopher started thinking about moving into politics as the old man started to withdraw from public life. The environment was a hot topic and his rising profile in the area would do him no harm at all. It was an image that he had encouraged, but it was not simply a public face. He did care about animals and the environment. And, in time, he would capitalise on this.

In fact, the time for him to step forward into what he called (in his speeches at any rate) "a life of service" came sooner than he had expected, with his father's death from a heart attack when he was only in his early sixties. Dede was dead too by then. It seemed to Christopher that everybody who mattered to him was dead. It was, of course, terribly sad, but also somehow liberating.

With his father's death it seemed natural to Christopher to take over the seat. In his mid-30s, good looking and with impeccable environmentalist credentials, he had been a shoo-in to succeed his father, so here he was: MP for East Richmond.

He had everything he had always wanted, so why was he feeling so stressed? Why did he feel that he was on the edge of losing the life he had built for himself?

That evening autumn had arrived. The trees in the park were bare and the cries of the rooks as they settled down for the night added a sinister feeling to the dusk. He would have to go home soon to strip off and wait for the moon to rise. Experience had taught him that even the most flexible sportswear could not survive the change from man to beast. Nudity was not a problem, though: nobody was going to see him.

The sun was sinking, but it was a cloudy night with no sign of a moon. In his melancholic mood, he did not want to turn for home yet. He drifted on through the park until he found himself at the Roehampton gate which led to the council estate that was the nearest the area came to a working-class district. Now he was an MP he supposed he should take more of an interest in the only significant council estate in his constituency. The estate, he knew, had been built at the end of the 1950s and was one of the largest in the country. He wandered around, staring up at the tower blocks which had been built on a Georgian landscape that mirrored the artificial beauty of the park next to it.

It was, he felt, a remarkable place – about as far from the conventional image of a council estate as could be imagined. How could he not have been here before? Just across the park from the home he grew up in, it was another world.

Fascinated, he lost track of time, exploring this alien place much longer than he'd intended. Long enough for the moon to rise. Stupid! Stupid! Stupid!

He barely had time to get into the shelter of one of the tower blocks before he could feel the change starting. And then came the hunger, overwhelming now.

He smelled the man before he saw him – the smell of sweat and drink and bad food and poor health. His meat would be rank and possibly not good for him, but his wolf brain did not care. Even the human part of him acknowledged its appeal. Like a greasy kebab at the end of a hard day, you knew it was bad was for you, but the sense of wrongness attached to it was a perverse part of what made it so very right.

He drew his lips back over his gums. The moonlight glinted on his canine teeth as he stepped out of the shadows.

* * *

He had, he knew, crossed a line.

Why? His father had controlled it and his father before him. Why could he not manage in his turn? Was he a failure – a disgrace to his family line?

He looked down at the body. Was it such a bad thing to have done? The man was a down-and-out. He would hardly be missed. And the thrill of the kill had been wonderful!

No, he was no failure! He had taken what was his birthright. It was his father and his grandfather who were the failures, denying their true natures, cravenly abasing themselves before the rules of a society that would never offer them the respect they deserved.

So he had killed a man. It was a spectacularly dangerous thing to have done. On the other hand, no one had seen him and the man was only some tramp. Would anybody really care?

He had loped back towards the park, keeping to the shadows. He had hardly slowed as he leapt the fence that marked the park boundary.

Now he was safe on land he knew well. Soon he was out of the park, moving through the shadows, back to the security of his home. He had got away with it.

They say that it's always the first time that's the hardest.

A month later he was running late. An important vote had kept him at the House. On the way home, he realised he wouldn't make it in time.

He asked the taxi to drop him at the World's End.

The second time was so much easier.

CHAPTER 5: Galbraith views a body

Galbraith had not looked forward to explaining to Supt Bailey that Pole was arranging for him to be seconded to Section S for the duration of the enquiry. Manpower (Galbraith still called it 'manpower' though he was getting better at not saying the word aloud) was always at a premium and Galbraith had expected Bailey to be out of sorts at the idea of losing his chief inspector. In the event, the superintendent took it philosophically.

"I'm going to have to get used to you going eventually and lending you to Section S may have its advantages. Nobody seems to know what it is they do exactly, but they have connections everywhere and if you work for them, I'm hoping some of those connections might be in a position to help me one day."

Galbraith made a non-committal noise. Although Section S certainly did have an extraordinary amount of influence, he had yet to learn any details of how it worked. The only Section S operative he had spoken to was Pole and Pole worked almost exclusively from his flat, which was notably lacking in any of the high-tech gimmickry that people like Bailey seemed to assume was available to a secretive department hidden away in Counter Terrorism.

"You'll have to get your new friends to supply any support you need, though. I can spare you at a pinch, but I can't spare anybody to staff up an Incident Room."

Galbraith nodded. Bailey could hardly be expected to provide resources to a unit that was officially nothing to do with him. Galbraith, though, was sceptical about any support coming from Pole's colleagues. As far as Section S was concerned, it seemed that the support being offered to Pole was to have Galbraith reporting to him. Handling the mechanics of a regular police investigation was not Section S's forte. Without resources from Bailey, Galbraith rather feared that he was on his own.

He made his way back along the corridor to his office, dodging a young civilian support worker pushing a trolley full of file binders towards the Superintendent's room – more papers to be added to the piles that Galbraith feared might one day collapse with dreadful consequences for anyone unfortunate enough to be sitting underneath them when they fell.

At least Bailey hadn't suggested that he should give up his office, so he had somewhere to make his personal headquarters.

He settled behind his desk and picked up the phone. The first step, he decided, was to establish himself as the centre for information about dog attacks.

When Galbraith had first joined the Metropolitan Police, he had held fast to the happy illusion that the various police stations scattered across London worked together as one well-oiled machine. It had taken two weeks and a single investigation into, of all things, a stolen bicycle for him to realise that nothing could be further from the truth.

There are 180 police stations in the Metropolitan Police district and it seems an article of faith in each of them that they should never communicate with any of the other 179. The bicycle was his own and it took those two weeks to establish that it had been recovered and was sitting in a police station only three miles from the one where he was based. The idea that its details might be circulated had never occurred to anybody.

Things had improved as far as bicycles went with a central computerised register. That was hardly likely to be the case with details of dog attacks. Pole simply shrugged when asked if Section S could help organise anything but, in fairness, they did throw their substantial political weight behind Galbraith's demand that any reports of deaths which might involve an attack by a dog or similar animal should be routed through to him.

Although Galbraith did keep paperwork in his office at Earl's Court, there was no question of running the investigation from there. This was Pole's case and Pole was not going to base himself in Galbraith's nick. The nearest that this investigation came to a central command and control centre was Pole's flat. It was more comfortable than the offices where Galbraith usually headed up investigations, but Pole insisted that the computer be hidden away in a Georgian cabinet when not in use and he would not tolerate a whiteboard under any circumstances. Galbraith felt strangely exposed without any of the bits and pieces he associated with a major enquiry, even if he suspected that some of them were essentially stage dressing rather than really necessary for the work to get done. He tried to spend at least a couple of hours every day in the mundane reality of his old office. It made him feel that this was, after all, a serious investigation of unexplained deaths rather than being caught up in a fantasy where perhaps the villain of the piece was a supernatural creature. The noise and camaraderie of the station reminded him that there was a normal world out there – something too easily forgotten in the half-light of a vampire's apartment. Even the appalling coffee and Sgt Green's sardonic remarks about "a wild ghost chase" were welcome.

Refreshed by his visit to the station, he would join Pole in his flat in the late afternoon. Pole was never at his best in daylight hours so this approach suited them both.

A few days went by with no further killings. As far as Galbraith was concerned that was good news. Perhaps the killings were unconnected and there would be no more. Perhaps the dog had died, or its owner was taking proper precautions to control it.

"Perhaps," Pole agreed, but it was clear that he did not believe it. "let's wait for the next full moon before we jump to conclusions, shall we? Hmmmm?"

Galbraith ignored his comments and his irritating vocal mannerism. He focussed instead on traditional police methods, clinging to them like a medieval peasant clinging to a charm in the hope that it might protect him against the powers of the supernatural. Once he had dealt with the bureaucracy of setting himself up as a clearing house for reports of dangerous dogs, he fell back on that old standard: the post-mortem. Death was due to exsanguination from a massive throat wound. The report drew no conclusions as to what might have caused the wound but it discounted an attack by any small mammal, such as a fox or a dog. There were minor puncture marks around the neck, in groups of four. The marks did not cause death. They were consistent with the wounds that might be caused by an animal but the distance between the marks would suggest a paw larger than that of any creature naturally found in the UK. The wounds could have been caused by a knife such as the tiger claw knife or *bagh nakh* of the Indian sub-continent, but the wounds were much less deep than would normally be expected from such a knife.

The post-mortem confirmed that there was flesh missing around the throat. There was also evidence that the ribs been cracked and that whatever had torn open the throat had removed some of the organs of the upper body through the wound. The pathologist had noted that part of the heart and lungs were missing. He had not speculated on where they had gone.

Once he had read the post-mortem report, Galbraith had pushed it to the centre of his desk, leaned back in his chair and sighed. He would have been happier if the pathologist had simply said "consistent with an attack by a dog," but he had notably avoided that. At least he hadn't said "consistent with an attack by a large mythical creature".

Galbraith was unwilling to admit that he was dealing with werewolf attacks until he had ruled everything else out. This was, as far as he was concerned, a regular police investigation of a suspicious death, so he treated it as such.

He checked the backgrounds of both men. No, they had never been in prison together; they had never shared the same night shelter; they had no friends in common. The only thing that linked them was the manner of their death and where their bodies had been found – dumped alongside the rubbish near high rise blocks of flats.

Galbraith followed up every report of a dangerous dog across London. The numbers shocked him. There are almost 2,000 dog attacks in London every year, but most were cases of children bitten in the street or dogs out of control in parks. None in the past three months had involved serious injury to a person, although there had been a report of a dachshund savaged to death the previous week. For a few minutes Galbraith had been delighted at the news, albeit sorry for the dachshund. The owner, though, had identified the killer as a bull terrier and Galbraith didn't believe that a dog that size – however vicious – could have brought down a man by ripping his throat out.

Perhaps the victims had, in a way, known their killers? Even a bull terrier could, he supposed, rip open the throat of anybody foolish enough to bend down to pet it. Did either of the men ever own a dog? Or have friends who owned dogs?

Neither man was what Galbraith might call gregarious, but anybody living on the street knows someone with a dog. Galbraith spent several days finding these people and their pets – generally skinny little creatures whose capacity for ripping the throats out of anything bigger than a rabbit seemed distinctly limited.

The dog – or whatever it was – seemed to have vanished. An interview with the Rangers' office at Richmond Park suggested that there wasn't even any sign that it had taken a deer that month.

After almost a fortnight, he was running out of possible avenues to explore. The next day he arrived at the office tired and irritated. His mood was not lifted by Sgt Green's cheery greeting: "Still working with the Loony Tunes?"

"For my sins."

Green was not involved in this case – in truth there was not really enough work for Galbraith – but he obviously had mixed feelings about his exclusion. On the one hand, he had made no secret of his distaste for Pole and Section S's way of doing things but, on the other, he resented the idea that Galbraith's relationship with Pole was closer than that with his sergeant.

"Any progress?"

"Remarkably little. Killer may have been a large animal or an unusually strong human with a taste of Asiatic knives and raw steak."

"Have you checked that the zoo isn't missing anything?"

"Next on my list."

Galbraith was lying. Until Green had suggested it, he hadn't considered the possibility. It was, he thought, unlikely that the Zoological Society of London had let a large carnivore escape and had neglected to inform the authorities, but there were private individuals who kept dangerous animals.

Back in his office with a mug of the station's usual apology for coffee, he ran a quick Google search for a register of dangerous animals in the London area. It turned out that no official register existed. Records of dangerous wild animals were kept by each individual local authority. Fortunately one of the animal charities that campaigned to set captive creatures free had collated all the information and presented it in a convenient map form. It didn't provide names and addresses but it did suggest that most London boroughs had no dangerous wild animals registered at all. There were a couple of Savannah Cats in Kensington. Galbraith thought of tigers and leopards but it turned out that Savannah Cats are a domestic cross and not much more than a foot tall. It seemed unlikely that they would be tearing the throat out of anything much bigger than a mouse. Somebody in Reigate had a pet crocodile, which seemed fairly alarming but it was hardly likely to be the killer in this case, unless crocodiles had leaping skills Galbraith was unaware of. The nearest wolves seemed to be in West Berkshire, which was unlikely but not impossible, he supposed. He was sure he had seen something about wolves roaming over hundreds of miles of Canadian forests. Presumably they could make it in from Newbury.

Half an hour on the phone to West Berkshire Council finally got him the address of the wolf-keeper and a short conversation with a rather worried council official who wanted to know why the police were interested in the Wolf Conservation Trust.

“We’ve had reports of a large wild animal in West London.” Galbraith saw no reason for going into more detail. "I just wanted to check that all of your wolves are where they are supposed to be.”

“Absolutely definitely, Chief Inspector. I check regularly.”

He sounded so concerned that Galbraith smelled a rat, but after several more minutes he established that the sensitivity was because the publicity that had surrounded a wolf escaping from the Trust back in 2018. Since then the Trust had improved its security and the council kept a close eye on it. If the mystery killer was a wolf, it hadn’t come from there.

Of course, Galbraith reflected, not everybody is careful to observe the law. If they did, he would be out of a job – but he couldn’t see anybody being able to keep a large carnivore in London without anyone noticing. Roehampton, though, was on the fringe of London. It was time to get back on the phone.

The problem with working with what Green had charmingly called ‘the Loony Tunes’ was that he had no junior staff around to do the leg work. The Metropolitan Police weren’t about to staff a murder investigation for what was, whatever Pole believed, officially a death ‘with no suspicious circumstances’. “Of course,” Superintendent Bailey had admitted on the one occasion that he had discussed the case with Galbraith, “there are plenty of things about it that are suspicious, but nothing which suggests a criminal act. I understand that the interest of Section S means we are unlikely to be looking for the sort of perpetrator who is going to end up in Brixton Prison. Hence, I’m afraid, no budget for a murder enquiry, so you are on your own.”

In many ways, Galbraith liked working without the energetic activity of enthusiastic young officers around the place, constantly reminding him that he was getting old and tired and cynical. But ringing every police station in Surrey to ask if anyone had reports of a large dog creating trouble in their area was not a particularly exciting way to spend his day.

He had decided to start with Inspectors at individual stations rather than asking further up the police hierarchy because it was unlikely that a nuisance dog was the sort of thing that would get reported up the chain of command. It turned out he was right. There were dogs that had stolen meat from a butcher’s; dogs that had been reported for keeping the neighbours awake barking at 2.00am; dogs that had been found abandoned; dogs that had been reported stolen; dogs that had caused road traffic collisions; dogs that had been injured in road traffic collisions. There were Corgis and Pekinese, Labradors and Collies, Lurchers and Newfoundland Rescue Dogs. All sorts and conditions of dogs had been caught up in all sorts and conditions of mischief. None, though, seemed likely to be of any interest to Galbraith.

When he met up with Pole that evening, his Section S colleague was unconcerned by his lack of progress. “Don’t worry,” he said, “less than two weeks to the next full moon and then we’ll have more to go on.”

Galbraith did not find this reassuring.

“Meanwhile,” Pole continued, “I’ve been pursuing my own investigations.”

“Amongst your nocturnal colleagues.”

Pole allowed his lips to curl ever so slightly. Galbraith realised that the vampire was seriously offended.

“Really, Chief Inspector, there is more to Section S than a network of informants amongst the Others: not to say that that isn’t useful, but we do have other resources.”

“You’ve been examining the scenes? Interviewing possible suspects?”

“Hardly. I rather imagined that is what you had been doing.”

Pole, it turned out had been reading. He had spent days trawling specialist bookshops and his copy of *De La Démonomanie des Sorciers* had been joined by various other volumes in French, Latin and what Galbraith took to be Greek. Pole kept searching through them, carefully turning pages so brittle with age that they seemed likely to crumble at his touch. “There are some key texts I can’t find,” he grumbled. “I fear I may need a trip to the British Library.”

“How do you propose to do that?”

“The Reading Rooms are open until eight. It’s not a problem, merely inconvenient.”

Galbraith spent the next day avoiding Sgt Green. The idea of investigating the supernatural was unsettling enough without having to deal with his sergeant’s facetious comments. He was even driven to asking Supt Bailey if there wasn’t some committee he could be sent to sit on. Bailey had grinned.

“You’ve changed your tune.” Then, more sympathetically, “No can do, I’m afraid. You’ve been seconded to Section S for the duration and that’s that.”

That evening, Pole seemed almost as dispirited as him. His trip to the British Library had, it seemed, been less helpful than he had hoped.

“The trouble is that the literature on lycanthropy is wildly contradictory. Older authors, like Bodin, generally view it as magical. Nowadays, of course, it's all seen as some sort of mental illness, though that does rather tend to skip over the whole 'changing into a wolf-like creature' element. There are suggestions that people imagine they have changed but that this is simply a delusion. As no-one has ever caught a werewolf for study purposes, it's all a bit conjectural for my taste."

"So where do we go from here?"

Pole poured another glass. He was making heaver inroads into the whisky than Galbraith had noticed before. This whole business seemed to be making the vampire uneasy.

"I rather fear that we wait. I think we can make little progress in the absence of more data and we will only get more data when the creature kills again. That suggests that we could occupy ourselves with other things until the next full moon. Maybe two nights before, just to be on the safe side."

"And then?"

"We put out extra patrols."

"There won't be funding for that."

Pole raised his voice slightly. Galbraith realised that the vampire was as angry as he had ever seen him. "Can your superiors not see the importance of this?"

"No," said Galbraith. "With all the problems London faces at the moment, the death of one more down-and-out is not going to be viewed by the powers-that-be as a policing priority."

Pole swept his hand out in a dismissive gesture. "It's not the victim I'm interested in. This is our chance to explore the unknown. We can move beyond the veil."

Galbraith put down his glass and looked hard at Pole. The vampire's skin was fractionally less pale than usual and Galbraith realised he had worked himself to a state in which, had he been wholly human, he would have been flushed with emotion.

"This isn't about solving the crime, is it?"

Pole recovered himself with a visible effort. "I take my responsibility to the police very seriously."

"But there's more, isn't there?"

Pole hesitated.

"This is between you and me," he said.

Galbraith nodded.

"For almost four hundred years we have kept our promise to the Crown. We move in the shadows, doing what the State demands of us. We have built up an organisation – Section S. It's small, but it reaches everywhere. We see things that no one is supposed to see. And we gather knowledge.

What do you think it's like, to be so different, hiding in plain sight in a world where there are more Mortals every year and we live in fear that you might one day turn against us and destroy us? You are many and we are so few.

For thousands of years humans have told stories of creatures from beyond the veil. Gods, demi-gods. Creatures monstrous and wonderful. Gorgons and dragons and unicorns. And vampires,"

He paused, as if disgusted with himself for having uttered that word.

"And we wonder, naturally enough, I think, if some of the other creatures are as real as we are. If we are not alone. Not so terribly alone."

* * *

The next day Galbraith sat at his desk unable to think of any way forward until Green pointedly suggested that if he had nothing to do, he might as well do it somewhere else. "You'll make no progress by sitting here and fretting," he pointed out, "and you're beginning to get on people's nerves. We have enough real criminals to worry about, without thinking that we might have to deal with things that go bump in the night."

He had a point, Galbraith felt. He would take the rest of the day off.

It had been a while since he found himself with a free afternoon in town. He shouldn't waste it. Perhaps he should play tourist. Like most Londoners, he hardly ever visited the famous sites of the city. He might as well start now.

He made his way to Regent's Park. It was nearby and the zoo was surely worth a visit, even though it was cold and there were only a few hours of daylight left.

He wandered towards the lions, guided by a vague memory of visits as a child. Hadn't there had been a lion house here once? There were still lions, but housed in some Indian-themed arena that he was sure was a new addition. Everything had changed. Galbraith sniffed to himself. He was, he realised, getting to an age where he found change a constant irritation. Shakespeare, as ever, had it right. He thought of Bianca's words in *The Taming of the Shrew*: "Old fashions please me best; I am not so nice To change true rules for odd inventions." What must it be like, he wondered, for Pole, watching the world changing around him while he remained forever the same?

He wandered on, still retracing his steps as a child. Now he was looking at goats and reindeer. Surely they had once had more interesting animals here. Suddenly he had a flash of the zoo as it had been when he stood, holding tightly to his father's hand and looking at something grey and dangerous and much more interesting than reindeer. Yes, the zoo had had its own wolf pack here but, it seemed, no more.

Had his unconscious memory guided him to where he could once have sat and watched the wolves? He shook his head and moved away towards the monkeys. He was beginning to grow a little too obsessive about wolves, natural or otherwise.

Pole, when, he told him how he had spent his afternoon, had laughed. "You're quite right. There used to be wolves there but now they've all been moved to Whipsnade. I remember when they first arrived and the novelty of hearing them howling across Regent's Park." He had at least recovered from the previous day's low spirits and when Galbraith admitted his conversation with Bailey, he was unsympathetic. "He's quite right. You're on secondment. You could have spent some time catching up with your reading on the world beyond the veil. Or, failing that, putting your feet up. There are alternatives to London Zoo. Have you considered the National Gallery?"

No, Galbraith had not considered the National Gallery.

"You should take your culture while you can. We're going to be busy enough when the full moon comes around."

"What exactly are you expecting then? Do you think we might catch him in the act?"

"It's unlikely. There's a lot of London and, if I'm right, we're dealing with a creature that is used to moving unseen through the night. And we mustn't forget that he's a powerful predator. The Others are strong, but I don't want to see if we can recover from the sort of damage he's likely to inflict. You did mention, I believe, that the post-mortem showed that the heart had been removed."

That was, Galbraith accepted, worrying. He tended to think of the Others as effectively invulnerable but rip out their hearts and they would be as dead as anything else.

"So what do you hope for?"

"Oh, you know," said Pole, airily, "clues."

"Would you care to be a little more specific?"

"Well …" Pole leaned forward, all trace of levity gone. "I'm thinking that this creature is based in the general vicinity of Richmond Park. Deer have been taken there every now and then for years. Then last month, for the first time, as far as we know, it moves out of the park – but only just out, to Roehampton. The next event is much further east at World's End. I think it's unlikely that he travelled from Richmond to Chelsea in lupine form – and if he was human, he was presumably wearing clothes. So when he transformed from human to wolf, he must either have taken his clothes off and put them away safely or he tore them off as he transformed and left the rags. In neither case is it likely that a wolf headed back across London with its clothes under its arm. So I want to get to the scene in time to find those clothes. If we can, it gives us real evidence that we are looking at a lycanthrope. Plus the clothes will offer the sort of physical evidence that might help identify our man."

"Or woman."

"Possibly. I appreciate that we must avoid sexist assumptions."

Galbraith decided to let that remark go.

"I can ring round stations in West London and ask them to keep a look out and let me know if anything comes up. There'll be no extra patrols though." He gave a wry grin. "Bailey says he's spent the last week explaining our manning and overtime levels to Deputy Assistant Commissioner Frontline Policing. I think it's his way of making sure I never ask for any extra patrols ever again."

"Well the Others will keep their eyes peeled too and one useful thing about Section S being tucked away in Counter Terrorism is that we have ready access to the CCTV network."

"Happy days, then." He raised his glass. "Here's to the next full moon."

* * *

In the end they didn't have a wait for the full moon. The third victim was found three days earlier than that. An anonymous phone call had reported a body in the bin area on the Abbots Estate in Pimlico.

It was 1.00 am so Galbraith had, reasonably enough, been at home. His request to be informed as soon as anything happened had been honoured. The station had even sent a car to collect him. They had blue-lighted to the scene but he was still unsurprised to find Pole there ahead of him. The vampire, presumably, had already been awake.

"Did any of your –" Galbraith paused, conscious that he might be overheard. "—associates spot anything."

Pole shook his head. "Alas no, Chief Inspector. And I understand that your more conventional colleagues spotted nothing either."

Galbraith shook his head. "No. It's a bloody good thing that some local citizen decided to do his civic duty and call it in. Otherwise the body could have been there until the bin men turned up. It's been a fair while since there were foot patrols on the Abbots Estate." He grimaced. "We'd best take a look."

They walked over to the bin area, tucked away at the foot of a block of flats, the scene illuminated by the strobing blue lights of a couple of police cars.

"If we're trying to find bits of clothing, we'll need a decent perimeter and some bodies out doing the searching. I'll make a start on organising that." Another car arrived and the police surgeon clambered out. Since Covid, the man had made a serious effort to lose more weight, but he still wheezed as he plodded his way to the body. Galbraith nodded towards him and said to Pole, "While I do that, see what you can get out of him."

Pole gave the slightest inclination of his head and turned away. Galbraith realised it was the first time he had ever ordered the man from Section S to do anything. After so long feeling like an assistant to his older colleague (several centuries older, Galbraith reminded himself) it was a refreshing change.

Organising the uniforms for the crime scene took a while. Galbraith was out of his area and had to make his peace with the local inspector, who was happy enough to send the men he asked for but unhappy to see their overtime charged to his budget.

"Counter Terrorism is paying." Galbraith hoped that Pole could tap into Section S's resources to come good on that promise or he was in trouble. An estate that hadn't seen a foot patrol for months was about to be overrun with police officers. Galbraith thought of the budget reports on Bailey's desk and winced. Tonight's effort was going to be paid for by a whole heap of minor crimes passing uninvestigated.

Pole left the police surgeon prodding cheerfully at the corpse and returned to Galbraith.

"I hope I didn't hear you spending my budget, Chief Inspector."

"Your hearing is very acute."

For a moment, Galbraith thought Pole was going to pursue the issue but then he gave a half-shrug and gestured in the direction of the corpse. "Rigor has barely set in, which puts the time of death around 11.00. He started with a lot of technical stuff about the cause of death but I could see for myself that the throat has been ripped open. It's almost beginning to seem like a pattern."

"Is this one homeless?"

"Identifying the corpse and digging up the details is more your area than mine, Chief Inspector. But taking a quick look, I'd hazard not. He seems clean, well shaven, and generally a step up from the last two bodies – but quite a small step. The residents on this estate are often living in somewhat straitened circumstances."

"You mean they're poor." He looked up at the tower blocks. "It's similar to Roehampton and World's End. Estate with tower blocks. Individual apparently indigent or poor."

Pole raised a hand to interrupt Galbraith's flow. "I hope I am not giving the impression that because they are poor, they do not matter. All were some mother's son. All must have been loved once, even if they are loved no more."

"Er, yes." Galbraith felt uncomfortable being lectured by a vampire on the respect he should accord to the victims. He did admit to himself that Pole was right though.

"We'll find out more about him in time. For now all we can say is that the body had its throat torn out and was dumped with the rubbish. I'm going to hazard a guess that the killer doesn't care that someone loved him once."

"Indeed." Pole's voice was dry. "There's the beginning of a geographical pattern too – starting at Richmond Park and moving progressively eastward."

There was silence while the two policemen tried to decide whether this was significant or not. Finally Galbraith spoke. "Let's try and see if we can find the clothing you predicted. That should at least give us an idea of whether or not we're on the right track."

A police van had turned up with half a dozen constables in it and Galbraith was soon directing them to seal off the whole area with yellow crime scene tape.

“What exactly are we after, sir?” The sergeant was young (though all sergeants seemed young to Galbraith these days) but he gave the impression of somebody who was very much on the ball.

"Clothing, sergeant: discarded clothing. It may be a neatly folded outfit or just torn scraps of cloth, but whatever it is we need it recovering and bagging. I want to know about anything else unusual but most of all I want to know whether we can find any clothing anywhere near the crime."

Galbraith realised that the uniformed officer wouldn't have seen the body yet.

"Don’t worry about the victim’s clothes. They are on what's left of the victim. We're looking for something that doesn't belong here."

The sergeant looked confused – as well he might, though Galbraith – but nodded and headed off to the newly arrived constables who were soon systematically working their way through the area.

Galbraith looked at his watch. 2.30 am. He yawned. Pole, of course, was wide awake.

“I thought I might call it a night. If they find anything, we can follow it up tomorrow.”

“As you wish, Chief Inspector. I think I will wait a little, if you don’t mind.”

“Suit yourself.” Galbraith knew he sounded ungracious. Let’s face it, he thought, he was being ungracious. It wasn’t Pole’s fault that he lived on a different sleep cycle to Galbraith.

He yawned again. And, gracious or not, he needed to get home.

He remembered that he had been driven over in a police car. His own car was outside his flat.

He looked about to see if there was anyone who might drive him back, but everybody was busy about the tasks that he had set them. He could hardly justify taking a man away to be his personal taxi service. Damn! That meant an Uber, and at this time of night he could expect a long wait.

He had just got his phone out to call a cab when a commotion near where the body had been dumped caught his attention. He put the phone back in his pocket and accepted that it was going to be a while before he got back to his bed.

One of the searchers was triumphantly holding up a raggedy piece of fabric. Other police officers were crowding round. Even after all his years with the force, Galbraith was always astonished by policemen's apparently primal need to group together whenever new evidence was turned up.

Pole was heading towards the centre of the crowd, which parted as if he were re-enacting Moses' trick with the Red Sea. Indeed, Galbraith thought, there was something almost Old Testament Patriarchal about Pole. His antique suit, his posture (which somehow made him seem taller than the Met Police's finest), the piercing eyes – all made Galbraith feel that, for once, Pole looked like what he was: an ancient creature from beyond our imagination and equipped with powers and knowledge the humans around him could never possess.

Pole reached out his hand imperiously and the scrap of fabric was handed over to him. He held it up to catch what light there was from nearby streetlamps and sniffed at it before starting back towards Galbraith while the sergeant ordered his men back to work.

Galbraith held up an evidence bag but Pole didn't immediately release the cloth.

"It's from a white shirt. Good quality. Whoever wore it was, I imagine, well-off. And…" He put the fabric to his nose and sniffed again. "Not quite human."

"You can tell?"

"Oh yes." Pole smiled, allowing a glimpse of very white teeth. "We are, in the end, predators. I know what a human should smell like and this is not a human."

"Any chance it's one of yours?" Galbraith was sure he knew what the answer would be, but he felt he still had to ask.

Pole's voice was cold. "No chance at all, Chief Inspector."

They had moved away from the others as they spoke, instinctively – it seemed to Galbraith – seeking the shadows.

"So you're confident it's a –"

"Werewolf. Yes, I am."

"And, if you're right about the shirt, it's a man. Probably rather a successful man."

"Indeed. Forensics might be able to tell you the size of the shirt, which will give us a useful indication of the size of the man. And there's always the possibility we will find more bits of clothing."

A shout behind them proved Pole right just as he was speaking. This time the scraps (there were several) were from trousers.

“Good quality again,” said Pole, with the confidence of a man who had been (albeit rather a long time ago, judging from the state of his suit) on first name terms with his tailor. “Slim, I’d say, even without a forensic laboratory’s assistance.”

“What do you think’s happened to the rest of his clothes?”

Pole pursed his lips. "Difficult to say. It may well be that some of his clothing was still clinging to his body when he made his way home – or wherever he went from here. Some of it will have been taken by animals.”

“Animals?”

“Certainly, Chief Inspector. This may look like a concrete jungle but there are plenty of creatures that will have been attracted by the smell of blood. Foxes, obviously, but also smaller creatures like rats. And we mustn’t forget domestic pets: dogs and cats may well be interested in blood-soaked clothing – although the smell of werewolf might put some of them off."

"There's no blood on the stuff we found."

"Precisely, Chief Inspector. But there will have been blood – a great deal of it, judging from the wound. Hence bloodied clothing. Yet we have not seen any bloodied clothing, hence my suggestion that animals may have taken it away.” He stopped, apparently struck by a new thought. “Could you ask your men to keep an eye out for shoes as well?”

The regular order of things, Galbraith thought, had been restored. He was, once again, Pole’s junior with the man from Section S effortlessly back in charge.

Galbraith could not say that he minded. In this strange world of supernatural beings, Pole’s knowledge was invaluable.

The shoes never did turn up and, sometime around four in the morning, Galbraith finally made his way to bed.

“I'll see you this evening,” Pole had said, bidding him farewell. “And we can toast our success to date.”

* * *

Galbraith didn’t meet Pole that evening. The forensic report had not yet turned up and, after a night without sleep, he decided that catching up on rest was more important. They would meet the next night and discuss progress then.

By the next night, though, there had been another death.

CHAPTER 6: In which our heroes investigate a fourth killing

Pole wasted no time on the niceties of polite conversation. "This one's different." His tone was grim.

"Different how?"

They were in a police car, siren wailing as it fought its way through the early evening traffic towards Vauxhall. One of Pole's watchers had called in the death at 6.45. Galbraith had still been in his office when Pole had rung him to say he needed to get to Vauxhall as quickly as he could. "Pick me up on your way," he had demanded peremptorily and hung up.

Hence the police car.

"It's too early in the evening."

"We've only had three and the only one where we have an approximate time of death was a couple of nights ago. What makes you say this one is too early?"

"It's barely dark. We know from accounts of the howling at World's End that the killing there was well after dark. Pimlico was about 11.00 pm. Roehampton may have been earlier, but we were working on the idea that he was hunting near his home territory, as it were, of Richmond Park. Which brings me to the second thing that is worrying me."

Galbraith said nothing. Pole would expound his theory whether he spoke or not.

"It's too far away. For years, as far as we know, this creature confined itself to Richmond Park. A couple of months ago it kills for the first time outside the park. We can put it down as a fluke, an accident, a momentary aberration. But then there is the killing at World's End. That's significantly farther from the park and constitutes a worrying trend – and a trend confirmed by the killing in Pimlico. Now, though, we have a death in Vauxhall. Pimlico and Vauxhall are separated by the river but are geographically adjacent. We cannot speak of a cluster of just two deaths, but this rather suggests to me that the creature has shifted, or is shifting, the base of its operations from Richmond to somewhere in the centre of town: somewhere with a notable absence of deer and rather a lot of humans."

They were heading towards Vauxhall Bridge, traffic pulling over at the sound of their siren.

Galbraith said, "It's a bit of a leap, isn't it? Two cases hardly prove anything and I'm not sure you have a valid point with the timing."

"Trust me on this. After 500 years one develops an instinct."

Galbraith nodded. He had a policeman's respect for "copper's nose".

The car was slowing now, pulling up behind two other police cars and an ambulance.

"Tower block again," said Galbraith. "He's consistent in that at least."

Pole nodded towards the ambulance. "I don't know why that's here. My source says he was very definitely dead."

"Routine. Somebody must have seen the body and dialled 999. An ambulance will have come out automatically." A couple of policemen were standing next to a man who was sitting on a low wall obviously very shaken. "That will be the guy who called it in. I don't suppose your source has stuck around to be interviewed?"

Pole shook his head. "He told me all that there was to know over the phone. 6.30; body dumped by bins; no sign of the killer. There was rather an odd smell, though. He's going to see if he can track it down. We're not very hopeful. We are particularly aware of odours but we're not bloodhounds."

"That's not a bad idea."

Pole gave Galbraith a glance that suggested he was having doubts about his colleague's sanity.

"Police dogs," Galbraith explained. "If the murder was recent, we can get dogs on the scent. We just need a rag of clothing."

He strode off to get a search started.

A police van arrived and more officers joined those already peering behind bins and fanning out around the tower block. A sign above the doors proclaimed 'Bannerman House'. As Galbraith returned, leaving a sergeant to pass on his orders, Pole gestured at the name of the flats. "It could be a military reference, I suppose. It's unlikely to be named for the vassal of one of the later shoguns. The best bet is that it's for Charles Bannerman who scored a century in the very first Test Match. We're close to the Oval, so that would make sense."

"Cricket fan, are you?" asked Galbraith.

"Hardly. I'm not really in a position to spend the long summer evenings sipping Pimms in a deckchair and listening to the thwack of leather on willow. No, my interest in Bannerman centred on his later life. He drank, you know, and gambled. It made him vulnerable to blackmail. By the time he played on the first official tour of England in 1878, he was accepting money from a foreign power. I pretend to be discreet, but I am sure you will understand that it could only have been Prussia. Anyway, his celebrity gave him access to a particular Royal Personage and he was able to obtain letters which, had they made their way to Prussia, could have been a source of embarrassment to the British government. I was asked to ensure that the papers were returned to the Royal Personage and I did so. Mr Bannerman was never allowed to represent his country again. It was quite sad, really."

Galbraith gave a polite shrug. There was, he thought, nothing that he could say.

Pole had apparently dismissed Bannerman from his mind and now watched the police activity like an ethnologist observing a previously undiscovered tribe. "So much commotion but I imagine it will take a while for them to organise themselves. Perhaps we might take a look at the body while we wait."

They walked towards the bins where a couple of men in the green overalls of the London Ambulance Service were waiting to be dismissed.

"Did you move the body?" Pole's question was abrupt and the taller of the ambulance men did not take it well.

"Of course we moved the body. We had to check for signs of life and we couldn't do that while he was in the dumpster."

Pole glanced down at the corpse which had been left on the ground where the ambulance men had placed it. There was the by now familiar wound in the neck.

"Couldn't you see the neck without moving him?"

"We have to check properly, not just take a glance into a dumpster and say that the guy seems dead."

Pole looked unimpressed and Galbraith hurried to defuse the situation.

"I appreciate your staying here. Can you tell us how the body was lying when you arrived?"

"It was dumped in that bin." He jerked a hand in the direction of the nearest dumpster. "The lid was closed but there was an arm sticking out. It was difficult to miss."

"That's really helpful." Galbraith had his notebook out and scribbled away. "If I can have your names in case we need to follow anything up, you can get off. And we are very grateful. Don't let my colleague upset you. He's having a bad day."

He shouldn't have said that, he knew. It was only that Pole's easy assumption of superiority verged on smugness and Galbraith welcomed this rare opportunity to put him down.

Pole watched the ambulance men move away before he spoke. "'Having a bad day.' Yes, I suppose I am. I apologise. I spoke out of turn."

And, just like that, the easy superiority was re-established. Galbraith felt like an ungracious oaf.

Pole turned thoughtfully towards the bins.

"In the previous killings the bodies appeared to have been dumped in bin areas because they were out of the way. They weren't exactly concealed, but the corpses were, shall we say, 'tucked away'. But the bins here are at the front of the flats and easily visible from the road."

"But lidded."

"Indeed. Which raises a couple of questions. Firstly, the lid was closed."

"To conceal the body."

"But the previous bodies, as we've just noted, weren't concealed. They were left behind bins or, in World's End, thrown on top of the dumpster. But here the body was placed *in* a dumpster and the lid closed. That suggests a more considered approach than previously."

"Perhaps he's learning to be more cautious."

"Then why leave an arm sticking out?"

Galbraith shrugged. "Carelessness? I don't know. Does it matter?"

"I think it might. I'm concerned that this creature is trying to send some sort of message. The body is worthless – something to be, as you say, 'put out with the trash,' but it wants us to know that it has killed. Far from trying to conceal the body, it leaves an arm exposed because it wants it to be found."

"Don't you think psychologically profiling a werewolf is a bit problematic?"

Pole turned to look again at the dumpster. He was, Galbraith thought, playing for time before replying.

"It's a werewolf, not a dog." Pole sighed. "We know very little about these creatures. Even in my community nobody has really taken the legends seriously. But these aren't zombies –"

"Wait a moment," interrupted Galbraith. "Are you telling me that there really are zombies?"

"Of course there are." Pole's tone was wearily matter of fact. "But can we keep to the subject at hand?"

Galbraith threw up his hands in a gesture of resignation.

"As far as we know, they can be as intelligent as they are in their human form."

"Then why the random killing and dumping bodies behind buildings? They don't give the impression of having carefully thought things through."

"I think that maybe they start at the mercy of their instincts – a primal need to hunt and feed. In time, though, as we see here, the creatures learn to master their urges. Now we see the human intelligence shine through."

Galbraith shook his head. "I don't think you have any evidence for that at all. You want to believe it's intelligent, so you're trying to find a pattern that isn't there." He turned away, attempting to disguise his irritation with Pole by snapping towards the search team.

"Have you found any fabric yet? The dogs should be here soon."

"No sign of anything. We're still looking."

Galbraith thought Pole's expression was unjustifiably smug.

"It doesn't prove anything. They're being slow. That's all."

"It's odd, though, don't you think? If there are no rags, he must have removed his clothing before he changed. Surely that suggests forethought and planning. And maybe even some control over the exact time that the change takes place."

"I thought it was when the moon rose. I suppose Google must be able to tell me."

"6.17 pm," Pole said. Part of Galbraith was delighted to see a human (more or less) who could make Google redundant, but part of him just thought Pole was showing off.

"So he might just have taken his clothes off at 6.15 and let nature take its course."

"Possibly," said Pole. "But many sources suggest that the moonlight has to be visible. It's quite a cloudy night. He can't have known that the moon would be shining."

"'Many sources.' Face it, Pole, it's all superstition and guesswork. You don't really know anything more about this creature than I do."

Pole tilted his head slightly and Galbraith felt that the man from Section S literally looked down his nose at him. "Then perhaps we could restrict ourselves to what you must accept are facts. If he has left no trace of clothing behind, he must have been naked. He arrived soon after dark. It is unlikely that he walked through Vauxhall in a state of undress. Ergo he must have taken his clothes off nearby. So perhaps you could spread your search further and see if you can find a bag or a case or something similar. Hmmm?"

The 'Hmmm,' Galbraith knew, was just added to annoy him. He was tempted to ignore Pole's idea but he recognised the wisdom of the suggestion. It would mean more searchers but it seemed that Section S's Counter Terrorist connections would find the budget so orders were sent out and another van of police officers arrived.

It was night by now. Away from the streetlights there were pools of darkness, pierced by the torches of the police searchers.

"Over here!" The cry came from a park a hundred yards or so down the road from Bannerman House. It was a little patch of grass with shrubs and trees relieving the gloom of the South London urban streetscape.

Pole never allowed himself to appear to be hurrying but, as Galbraith knew from their walks together, he moved with deceptive speed and he arrived in the park well ahead of Galbraith.

One of the constables was pointing at a clump of bushes. The torchlight was reflecting off the plastic of a cheap sports bag.

"Better get a photographer over. Forensics might as well make themselves useful." Galbraith called. Forensics had finally arrived but, with the body already moved, had been left with little to point their cameras at.

A policeman detached himself from the crowd gathering in the park and hurried back to Bannerman House to get the crime scene technicians.

Pole was already crouching next to the bushes and reaching for the bag. Galbraith bent next to him. "Can't you wait?" he hissed, not wanting to be seen rebuking a senior colleague in front of the uniforms clustered around.

Pole ostentatiously removed a pair of police issued rubber gloves from his coat pocket. "See. All done by the book."

"But the photographer ..."

"Will feel very stupid if the bag is just some teenager's football kit." He tugged at the zip. "Ah!" he said. "Definitely not a football kit."

The photographer had arrived and Pole reluctantly moved aside while he took several shots of the bag where it lay. Only then did Pole lift it carefully out of the bushes and finish unzipping it. As the photographer busied himself clicking away, Pole removed a white shirt, a dark suit, a tie, underwear, and a pair of shoes.

Galbraith drew a sharp intake of breath. "Well if these are here, what the hell is he wearing now?"

"A good question." Pole picked up the shirt and fingered the fabric. "The scraps we found in Pimlico were high quality. This is cheap." He looked at the jacket. "This too." He dropped it back into the sports bag with an expression of distaste. "It's as if they were bought to be disposable – almost as if he expected to abandon them."

"In which case he's presumably running around naked."

"It would seem so." Pole picked up the shirt and pressed it to his nose. "There's practically no scent. I would say it has hardly been worn. I doubt the dogs will have enough to go on."

"I'd hope we can find a naked man in Vauxhall even without the dogs."

"If he's not come back to collect the clothes that's because he is still in werewolf form." Pole gestured at the park around them. "Even in the city there are lots of bits of parkland. There are railway tracks that he can follow out. It's dark. Even if someone saw him from a train, they'd likely think they were imagining it. London isn't a concrete jungle. There's a surprising amount of open land. And further out there are gardens. If he's still in his non-human form he'll be able to hurdle across fences and hedges. If people catch a glimpse, they'll think it was a fox. People see what they expect to see."

"So we're no further forward."

"We know a little more than we did. We don't know the man's face but we do know now that it definitely is a man." He picked through the clothes. "Around six feet tall, reasonably slim build. And the choice of a dark suit suggests that he's not particularly young."

Galbraith, who had been crouched alongside Pole, stood and turned around, peering through the darkness at the scrap of parkland and the bushes where they had found the bag. "So he comes here wearing the clothes and hides in the park, takes them off and puts them neatly in a bag. Why?"

Pole looked thoughtful. "I suppose he could just be a naturally tidy sort of person. I have to admit I would find it difficult to simply throw my clothes onto the ground, even in the unlikely situation of feeling the need to undress in the open."

Galbraith struggled not to grin. The thought of Pole stripping off in a park was difficult to imagine.

"Even so," Pole continued, "bringing the bag suggests he had given it some thought. I'd really like to know what was in his mind."

CHAPTER 7: In which Garold believes

Like many politicians, Garold gave the impression that he was not prone to self-doubt. It wasn't true, of course. Even the most muscularly self-confident have their moments of doubt. In his case, these would tend to come in those nights when he woke, suddenly and unexpectedly, at about four in the morning. One of the incidental benefits of the night of the full moon was that he would be in wolf form at 4.00 am and wolves do not have any self-doubt at all.

A psychologist would have had no trouble in tracing Garold's insecurities back to his childhood. His grandfather's influence meant he grew up in a family where failure was inconceivable. His father's attempts to please Dede with his political success were doomed. When he was first elected, Dede assumed that within months he would be a minister and when this took (as was to be expected) almost two years, Dede made it clear that this was not what was expected of a Garold. Once he was a minister, Dede wanted to know why he was not in Cabinet.

It was hardly surprising that Christopher's father had little time to spend meeting the emotional needs of his child, and his wife's death while Christopher was still young made things worse.

It was not that Christopher was not loved. Both his parents and his Grandfather did love him – but they struggled to show their love in a way that could help the child. What they did show – more than they realised – was that, as a Garold, Christopher, like his father and his grandfather before him, was destined for success. Christopher, then, grew up knowing that great things were demanded of him and that he could expect no help from others in achieving them.

It was probably inevitable that, even if his father had not been a Conservative MP, Christopher would have been attracted to the Conservative party. True to his grandfather's view of the world, he believed that people were limited only by their imagination and their willingness to apply themselves. Dede had, after all, arrived from Turkey with nothing and had built up his wealth by hard work and application. If he could do it, anybody could.

Christopher Garold did not think of his approach to politics as cruel or uncaring. As he continually demonstrated in his constituency work, he was always ready to help those who he believed were let down by society through no fault of their own. When it came to people who were simply sponging off the State, though, it was a different matter. He was a strong supporter of cuts in benefit for the unemployed. He wanted more, and stricter, tests to ensure the disabled really were disabled. And he saw no reason why old people should get any form of assistance from the state while they still had savings. He was often on his feet in the House of Commons to give vociferous support to the latest efforts of the government to clamp down on what he always thought of as the undeserving poor. "Far too many people," he thundered, "blame others for their problems when, with a bit of will power, they could overcome the things that stop them becoming useful members of society."

Sometimes, in the small hours of the night when doubt snuck in through the cracks in his psyche, he wondered if it could be as simple as that, but by morning he would have convinced himself again that we all the masters of our fate. And, in case he ever had a moment of uncertainty that life could really be that simple, he had a motivational poster on his wall. 'If you BELIEVE,' it said in bold, bright colours, 'you can do anything.'

The morning after his expedition to Vauxhall he sat in his office in Portcullis House staring at the poster. He had managed to control the time that he switched, keeping himself in human form after the moon had risen, albeit for only ten minutes or so. He had believed and, by sheer force of his will, he had succeeded. It proved it could be done though and he was sure he could learn to control it better. The problem had been getting back to normal afterwards.

The trip home to Richmond had not been fun. It was a long way, for one thing. Even werewolves get tired. And it hurt his pride, skulking in gardens, scurrying along railway lines. He wasn't an animal like the foxes and rats that he had shared the night with. It was not fitting that he was reduced to this. Hunting in Richmond Park and loping home through the trees had felt noble and liberating, but not this. This was, he felt, quite sordid.

Perhaps he should stop. Perhaps it would be wiser to kill close to home and stick with the deer. After all, deer had sufficed until now.

No: he could never go back to that now he knew the thrill of real hunting. It was intoxicating. Much better than drugs. (He had never really seen the appeal.) Better even than sex.

It wasn't the killing or the eating. There was pleasure in stalking a deer and food, when all was said and done, was just food. It was the power.

People claimed to go into politics for all sorts of reasons: to make the world a better place; to help their fellow man; because of a sense of duty to their country. But in the end, people went into politics for the power. That sense that their lives were somehow bigger than those of the little people. They might – often did – exercise that power for good. Christopher Garold had spent hours sorting out some constituent's housing problems when the local authority had failed to fix a leaky boiler that could well have ended up dangerous. He had led a protest against cuts in suburban train services and the locals who had found their journeys to work that little bit easier as a result had been grateful. He had even spoken out on TV against the use of tropical hardwoods in furniture manufacture and was still the darling of the environmental movement.

Exercising power like this was gratifying, of course, but it was ultimately unsatisfying. Had he really gone into politics to sort out problems with boilers? If that was what he wanted to do, shouldn't he have taken up plumbing?

What he felt when he was hunting – that was real power: power in its purest form. Casting aside the trappings of civilisation, stalking naked through the city, hunting his prey and taking: taking life, taking the heart, taking whatever he chose.

They loved him in Richmond East. His constituents thought he was a good man. He heard them talking about him. (He had exceptionally good hearing, even in his human form. It served him well.) His name came up as couples took lazy brunches in local pubs, flicking through the Sunday papers. "He may be a Tory, but his heart's in the right place." They liked that they could have the benefits of his government's policies ("Lower taxes," he liked to say, "are good for everyone") without feeling they had voted for an MP they would have to feel guilty about. "Say what you like," he had heard somebody say when he was admiring the children's paintings at the school fete, "but he really cares about environmental issues."

The whips had been worried at first. Rumours had reached him through the grapevine that linked the Commons tea rooms and the Members' Bar and the cafeteria in Portcullis House. "They say he's not too sound. I mean all that environmental, caring staff was alright under Cameron, but times have changed," and people would tap their noses and look at him meaningfully. Nobody ever said exactly what they thought anywhere in the Palace of Westminster. You never knew who might be listening.

The whips had nothing to fear, though. Garold was all-too-aware of the Government's wafer-thin majority and had no intention of rocking the boat. He could be as hard-line on cutting benefits or closing day centres as anybody in the party. The trick, he had realised, was to make criticisms general but praise specific. He was always the first to volunteer at a food bank and whenever there was a reporter there to photograph his efforts – and there always did seem to be a reporter there – he would be overheard praising the efforts of the person who was collecting the food she needed. (It was usually a woman, preferably an attractive woman who would look good in the photo.) His praise would, by implication, contrast her with the good-for-nothing idlers whose laziness meant that funds that should have been available for people like her had been siphoned off by those who didn't deserve society's largesse.

He had joined the Conservatives because the idea of his taxes subsidising lazy people who didn't contribute to society was personally abhorrent to him. His father and grandfather had worked hard and amassed substantial fortunes and he saw no reason why he should be paying taxes on the family's money to benefit people like… Well, like the people he hunted.

People in the party were always talking about ridding society of the idlers, the scroungers, the ne'er-do-wells. And now they had elected someone who was doing what they had asked for.

He couldn't stop now. He must learn to control his power. He must be that remarkable thing: an MP who would give his voters exactly what they wanted.

The problem with changing from werewolf to human was that exercising any control at all called for a significant mental effort. As a young man he had visited an ashram in Nepal. (It was a gap year thing: virtually a rite of passage in the circles he had moved in.) He had learned to enter a meditative state that allowed him to control his body to what seemed at the time a quite astonishing degree. He could raise or lower his pulse. He could breathe so gently, holding his breaths so long, that he appeared dead. It was by entering such a trance state that he could control the change from human to werewolf.

There was no chance, though, of his working the same trick travelling in the opposite direction. He was beginning to exercise more control in his werewolf form – he thought the idea of dumping the body in the bin made his feelings about these people clear. He was choosing his victims more carefully too. He did not just feed opportunistically on drunks that he happened across. Apart from anything else, drunks tasted terrible. No, he was hunting round council estates, looking for people who lived on handouts: the jobless, the workshy. He could smell it on them. It was the smell of poverty and failure, and in ridding society of such people he was achieving more than he could ever achieve in parliament.

He could not, though, hope to enter a trance state while he was still a hunting animal with the taste of blood in his mouth.

Could it be that it was impossible? Could it be true that the legacy of his wolfishness, passed down from father to son, was indeed, as it was so often called by those who wrote stories about it, a curse: the curse of the werewolf?

He looked again at the poster on his wall. 'If you BELIEVE, you can do anything.'

There had to be an answer.

* * *

It was a very different sort of poster that gave him the solution to his problem. In recent years there had been some well-publicised cases of MPs who had responded to the stress of their job by getting uproariously drunk and then, depending on what sort of MP they were, either getting into brawls with passing journalists or indecently assaulting their staff. The response of the House authorities had been to allocate an office conveniently hidden deep in the bowels of the Palace of Westminster where MPs could seek professional help for their emotional crises.

'Struggling with stress?' the poster in the Portcullis House foyer asked, before offering its solution: 'Seek confidential help in room 537. Call the helpline now.'

Well, Garold thought, he was definitely struggling with stress.

He was not a great fan of counselling. Given the damage his family had inflicted on him, he might well have benefitted from it, but it was not an idea he would ever have entertained. In fact, he had opposed the setting up of the counselling service in the House. But he remembered that the counsellors could arrange an appointment with a psychiatrist – and a psychiatrist could prescribe medication. If he could convince the shrink that he needed something to calm him down, then maybe he could keep the werewolf under control. It was, he decided, worth a shot.

CHAPTER 8: In which Galbraith enjoys an omelette

With nothing to offer the dogs to give them the scent of their target, the search was not a success.

"The one thing everyone seems agreed on," said Pole, "is that werewolves are fast. By the time the dogs arrived he was probably halfway to Richmond: that's if he's still based in Richmond."

They were in Pole's flat again. Pole had poured a particularly generous measure of whisky and was whipping up another omelette. "I wondered about something more adventurous," he said, "but you seemed to enjoy it so much last time."

Galbraith nodded his appreciation. Pole was clearly on best behaviour after the tetchiness that both of the detectives had been showing over their last few meetings. Galbraith wondered what was giving rise to these tensions. Werewolves were obviously outside his comfort zone, but they seem to be worrying the vampire as well.

Pole spoke as he flipped over the omelette. "You said you've identified the victims."

"Yes. They're not down-and-outs like the first two. Both were unemployed and living on benefits but they had flats on the estates where the bodies were found. The Pimlico victim was Dave Miller. He lived alone in a flat there. It's almost impossible for a single man to get social housing nowadays but he'd been there for the past twenty years. Never held a job all that time, as far as we can see. He'd been pulled in a couple of times for minor assaults, but nothing dramatic. Neighbours said he was a nice guy, helped out when he could. I'd say he was generally well-liked but a bit of a loser."

Pole served the omelettes. "It's a good thing I'm confident about the werewolf hypothesis because I have to admit that he is exactly the sort of person who is targeted by some of the more irresponsible elements in our community."

Galbraith took a mouthful of omelette and chewed carefully. It was delicious and, more importantly, meant that he could not be expected to respond to Pole's remark.

After a brief pause for appreciative noises about the food, he continued.

"The man in Vauxhall was also a David – though I think we can discount that as a link. Dave Everett. He had a flat in Bannerman House on account of he has a wife and a young daughter, so that makes him a priority for social housing. Which is a good thing because he would never be able to afford to live in Vauxhall otherwise. Jobless for the last ten years."

"And the wife?"

"She works. I went to see her and I got the impression that she is what keeps the family together. She certainly didn't seem overwhelmed with grief about his death. He didn't seem to contribute a lot." Galbraith thought about the flat, tiny but clean and neat. Even while he was there, Mrs Everett was busy washing up, attacking the dirty dishes as if they were somehow responsible for the size of her flat, the squalor of the estate and the inadequacies of her husband. Her daughter was still up, although Galbraith was sure that she should have been in bed long since. Unlike her mother, whose face showed only bitterness and anger, the little girl looked as if she had been crying and was struggling to come to terms with grief. Perhaps he was judging her father too harshly. "His daughter will probably miss him."

Pole did not respond. He had served most of the omelette to Galbraith and now he finished his own small portion and arranged his silverware neatly on the empty plate before speaking.

"So there is a definite pattern now: unemployed males in council estates."

Galbraith took another mouthful. It really was, he thought, an excellent omelette. Reluctantly he dragged his mind back to the victims.

"It's certainly the case so far."

"It makes me wonder if there may be some sort of political point being made."

Galbraith dabbed at his lips with the napkin that Pole had set beside his plate. In his house, kitchen towel did the perfectly adequately, but a linen napkin, he admitted to himself, added a touch of class.

"What makes you say that?"

"Well, to be blunt, I probably know more than you about the odds of killing random strangers on the streets of London and discovering them all to be long-term unemployed. Unemployed, maybe: times are hard. But not unemployed for decades."

Galbraith decided not to think about how Pole gained this experience.

"So you think he's killing the unemployed because… Well, why exactly? Because he's on a crusade against benefit scroungers?"

"Stranger things have happened," said Pole.

"So we're looking for a well-dressed male about six feet tall. I suppose it's fair to say that he's unlikely to be a Guardian reader. Perhaps we should start checking on known right-wing extremists."

Pole raised an eyebrow. "The Home Secretary is on a crusade against benefit scroungers. I think you'll have to cast your net a little wider than the lunatic fringe."

"Well without that, we have even less to go on."

"You're forgetting location. Long-time West London resident probably now living or working in the Vauxhall/Pimlico area."

"That's still a few hundred thousand people."

"It won't be as many as that. And we can rule out cat owners." Pole's tone was dead-pan and Galbraith had no idea whether he was joking or not.

"We can put extra police patrols on council estates in central London, but we're not going to get anywhere until he's killed again – unless one of your network sees him on the prowl. Perhaps we ought to warn people to be on the lookout."

"I think not. 'Serial killer on loose: police achieving nothing' is not a headline designed to reassure the public."

"I'm surprised the press hasn't got hold of it though."

"Are you really?"

Galbraith looked at Pole's carefully neutral face and was again impressed by how far Section S's tentacles penetrated. After all, if you could keep the existence of an entire population of vampires out of the media, concealing a single werewolf must be child's play.

Pole took away the plates, returning to the table with a cheese board. "I've put out some cheddar. You look like a cheddar man. But there's rather a nice Stilton and some interesting goat's milk offerings."

Galbraith was indeed a cheddar man and attacked the familiar yellow block with relief. Goat's milk cheeses, he felt, might suit foreigners, but they were not for him. He cut a solid chunk and chewed it thoughtfully before speaking.

"I feel uncomfortable doing nothing, but I think we'll be waiting a month now before he kills again."

"Possibly," agree Pole. "But that part of the pattern has definitely been broken. I worry that he might be less controlled by the moon than we might wish."

CHAPTER 9: In which Garold seeks professional help

Garold had wasted no time in getting an appointment with the counselling service. He'd called late on Friday once he was at home. It wasn't a call he wanted to make from the office. In theory his privacy was well protected there but, ever since Matt Hancock's unfortunate carelessness with a surveillance camera, Garold, like many of his colleagues, preferred to do anything really confidential outside the Palace of Westminster.

He rehearsed before the call, checking how he looked in the bathroom mirror. He'd read that your expression reflects in the voice you use on the phone, so he'd practised with a hangdog look quite unlike the confident face he usually showed the world. When he got through, he had sounded convincingly depressed with a slight tremor in his voice that suggested a terrible underlying tension.

The young woman he spoke to had seemed very apologetic about not being able to offer him an appointment until Monday morning.

"Of course, if it's urgent …"

She was obviously concerned that this might be another MP about to go spectacularly off the rails over the weekend but Garold had assured her that he could cope until Monday. The plan depended on his seeming like someone who needed help dealing with stress but not someone who couldn't be trusted with their own medication.

The hardest bit of getting that first appointment was finding Room 537. When people said that it was hidden in the bowels of the palace, they weren't joking. It turned out to be in a corridor leading from the cellar which was ritually searched by Yeomen of the Guard every year on the anniversary of the Gunpowder Plot. Perhaps, Christopher Garold thought, if poor Guido Fawkes had had the benefit of counselling services, he wouldn't have felt the need to blow up Parliament.

Garold had spent an hour or more on Google researching his symptoms and, once he had located Room 537, he had no problem convincing the earnest young counsellor that he needed more than a shoulder to cry on and a few reassuring words. He needed, at the least, something to help him sleep. That meant a prescription, so he was booked in to see the psychiatrist on

Wednesday. There he explained again about his panic attacks and struggles to sleep. He was confident that he sounded convincing – so convincing that he almost believed in them himself. He needed, he explained, something to break the cycle of a poor night's sleep followed by anxiety, followed by a panic attack and another night tossing and turning. The psychiatrist started to explain that he would be prescribed Valium but Garold insisted he had taken Valium before. (It was true: he had, like many students, taken it in the weeks ahead of finals and this was duly recorded in his medical notes.) He wasn't looking to take drugs over a long period – just a short course of something powerful to get his sleep back on track. He was sure he had heard of something: "Clone-something-or-other, doctor. One of the guys on the other side was given it and swore it sorted him out." It was, Garold reckoned, a safe bet that at least one Labour MP had been prescribed it and professional ethics meant the doctor couldn't ask who. It was a nice touch, too, making it a Labour MP. Nobody would admit weakness to anyone on their own side of the House. This was the sort of secret you would only share with a political opponent.

"You're probably thinking of Clonazepam," said the doctor.

"That might have been it," Garold said with a careful hesitancy. He didn't want it to be too obvious that that was exactly the drug he had come in to get.

"It's powerful, but …" The doctor hesitated.

Garold allowed a tiny tic to flicker on his face: nothing too obvious. "I think I need something quite strong, doctor."

"It's certainly strong. It will help you sleep and control panic attacks, but the effects can last six to twelve hours. You'll feel sleepy and clumsy. We could start you on something a little less potent…"

Garold interrupted. "Clonazepam is safe, though, isn't it?"

The doctor insisted, as Garold had known he must, that the drug was safe. "In the right dose. Used with care."

Garold kept the anxious look on his face, but inside he was triumphant. "So you could prescribe it."

"Well, yes but…"

"Oh, thank you, doctor. I'm sure that's the answer."

The doctor hesitated. Just one more nudge, thought Garold. "You know, I was against setting this service up. Quite a few of us were. But now I realise what a mistake that was. I'll make sure my colleagues do too. We should be expanding this facility, not trying to cut it back."

This was the first the doctor had heard about people trying to cut funding for counselling. (This was hardly surprising, as the idea was entirely Garold's invention.) But obviously the counselling service needed all the friends it could get. And, as he had assured his patient, the drug was safe.

It took another ten minutes of lectures, questions about his drinking and a check on his weight (he enjoyed that bit: he was trim for his age and liked to show that off) and then he was back in the cellars, a prescription clutched triumphantly in his hand.

* * *

The whole process was, he admitted, almost terrifyingly efficient: it suggested that the counselling service had rather too much experience with over-stressed MPs. Even so, by now the full moon had been and gone. It was almost a week past the full and he was not at all certain that he would be able to change. Since he had been exercising more control in his werewolf form, he felt that he was able to choose, up to a point, when he changed from human to wolf. He would not allow his condition (as he thought of it) to control him as it had when he was younger. Now he would control it. Every morning, as he brushed his teeth, he would look at himself in the mirror and recite his new mantra, 'If you believe, you can do anything.' Admittedly it came out more as 'ifubereeoocandoanytin' but his dentist would have understood. It was, in any case, the thought that mattered.

On Thursdays, the House of Commons sitting day ends at 5.30. Thursday night, he decided, would be the ideal time to test whether or not the drugs would work.

He'd bought another cheap suit and two sports bags. With the aid of the drugs he hoped to be able to get back to human form and retrieve the clothes. The House of Commons to Victoria Station is a short walk. He left Westminster wearing his usual smart suit and carrying the other one in one of the sports bags. He was not going to be seen leaving the House as anything other than his usual immaculately dressed self. Christopher Garold in a cheap suit would definitely draw attention and this evening he was determined not to stand out in any way.

At Victoria Station he went into the toilets where he changed his clothes, leaving in the cheap disposable outfit with the smart suit in the second sports bag. That bag went into left luggage and he took the train to Clapham Junction.

In keeping with his ambition to take control of his situation, he had planned his route with care. From Clapham Junction he walked to the football changing rooms on Clapham Common. In the dark of the Thursday evening, they were not in use. He had brought a stout screwdriver with which he jemmied the lock. He stripped and then, having packed the clothes into the sports bag, he slipped out of the changing rooms and hurried to bushes nearby, concealing the bag before hurrying back inside. He was pretty sure that nobody had noticed him. It occurred to him that, given the reputation of Clapham Common, anyone who did see a naked man there might not think it that remarkable.

Now he had to wait for the moon to rise. With the date being well past the full moon, he did not think that there would be a spontaneous change. But he was sure he could make it happen. He imagined that motivational poster again. He believed. He could do it.

Hidden away in the changing rooms he waited, thinking about the change, thinking about wolves, thinking about his plans for the evening.

Nothing.

Time passed and with it came a growing frustration. How could this be happening to him? Had the motivational poster been wrong?

More time passed and the frustration began to turn to anger.

For a moment, he felt his skin crawling; felt muscles flexing; sensed a change deep inside his bones.

It was happening.

Relief flooded his system and, in the same moment, he felt the changes stop. He remained human and there was no sign this would change.

What had he been thinking when the change had started? What had triggered it?

He looked out the window. There was the moon: clear and bright, certainly, but definitely beginning to wane. The frustration surged again and again there was the sense of a change in his body. The muscles under his skin twitched and swelled as his frustration grew. It was, he realised, as simple as that. In the same way that the drugs would calm him so that he might be able to change from werewolf to human, so it was his frustration and – more importantly – his anger that was initiating the change from human to werewolf.

Using the same techniques that he had learned to force his mind into a state of calm, he now concentrated on his anger. He thought of all the things that he hated about the world he lived in: the drug-addled youths, the work-shy young men and their sluttish women, the ignorant and the stupid, asylum seekers, foreigners generally, and, for some reason, the Welsh.

He felt the anger build and the change beginning, but he remained stubbornly human: a rather hirsute human with disturbingly long fingernails, but human nonetheless. It only needed one last effort. He pushed open the door and threw himself out of the hut. He imagined he could feel the rays of the moon on his naked body. Just in time, he remembered to swallow the clonazepam that he had been prescribed. It should take effect within half an hour, but he reckoned that in werewolf form it was likely to take longer. It should, in any case, give him time to do what he had planned.

Even as he swallowed the pill, he felt his human side being submerged. It was all he could do not to howl at the moon. Instead he forced himself to head north, across the railway lines towards the Winstanley Estate and the 17 storey Inkster House.

CHAPTER 10: In which there is a fifth killing

When the full moon came and went with no more bodies turning up, Galbraith felt that it was safe to relax for another month. With Section S insisting on a news blackout, there was little they could do. The extra police patrols around high rises on council estates had been withdrawn. Even with Counter Terrorism's budgets, the police didn't really have enough people to maintain that effort for long and the increased police presence was already leading some community groups to complain that working class districts were being harassed.

Bailey had relented and agreed that he could fill the periods of inactivity in his investigation by doing other work – but, he insisted, not involving himself with other cases. "You can't dip in and out of ongoing investigations. You know better than that." So Galbraith found himself back in a world of Excel spreadsheets and strategy meetings with titles like 'Police Priorities in a Post-Covid Age' and 'Engaging Synergies in Diverse Communities'. At least, he thought, it meant almost a month of regular hours. He had even decided to buy an omelette pan and see if he could bring his kitchen skills up to Pole's level.

He was at home by 7.30 on Thursday night and was browsing Netflix with a freshly opened beer to hand when the phone rang.

As soon as he heard Pole's voice, he knew it was bad news.

* * *

The car that was taking them to Clapham was crossing Battersea Bridge as Pole summarised the new murder.

"Basically it's a repeat of Vauxhall. South of the river; tower block. It's actually owned by Wandsworth, as was the one in Roehampton. I suspect that has no significance. The body was found in a dumpster but one arm sticking out to make sure we get the message."

"Early evening again."

"Indeed." Pole sounded weary.

"We'll need a fingertip search around the flats, though I'm not very hopeful. And then a wider search in case he's left clothes behind."

"As you will doubtless be using my budget, I took the liberty of getting Section S resources on it."

Galbraith gave him what he was old enough to consider 'an old-fashioned look'. "And these resources will be better than our search teams how, exactly?"

"I didn't say 'better,' Chief Inspector. But they may bring some, shall we say, 'special skills' to the effort."

They swung into the Winstanley Estate, pulling up behind half a dozen police cars, their blue lights strobing across the scene. As they got out of their car, an unmarked black van with a blue beacon magnetically clamped to the roof pulled up beside them.

"Excuse me," said Pole, "I need to speak to my colleague."

Galbraith was curious as to who this colleague was and what, or who, was in the black van, but Pole's attitude discouraged curiosity and, in any case, a van filled with more conventional police officers was stopping behind them in its turn. Galbraith decided to brief his search teams first and to worry about Pole's associates later.

* * *

In the end, the most important evidence came from neither of the search teams but from one of the officers door-knocking in the tower.

"I think you should come and hear this, sir."

Constable Finnis had only been in the force for three months and her manner suggested she was not used to talking to chief inspectors, but she had clearly thought whatever she had found was important enough to bring straight to him.

They took the lift to the 17th floor. Galbraith, who had travelled in more than his share of council block lifts over the years, was impressed. It was smart and clean and there wasn't the faintest trace of urine in the atmosphere.

Finnis, whose station covered the estate, noticed Galbraith's expression. "A lot of the flats have been sold off," she said. "You can get close to half a million for them. That sort of money buys a lot of lift engineers."

The door to Flat 172 was a deeply stained stripped wood, not like the standard painted doors on the flats either side. Galbraith recognised the obvious sign of a flat that had been bought from the council.

The owner was Alex. He worked in IT, he said, and had been born in this block. He had inherited the tenancy from his parents and bought the place soon after.

"Nice place to live?"

"Very nice. The area's going up in the world."

"My officer here tells me you had a bit of trouble earlier this evening though."

"Not trouble exactly. She asked me if anything unusual happened and I told her about being threatened by some big dog."

"Threatened?"

Alex shifted uneasily. "Well, it felt threatening."

"So what exactly happened, sir?"

"I got home about quarter past seven. The front door downstairs is supposed to be kept locked and tonight, for once, it was. So I had to get my keys out and I suppose I was fumbling to find them because usually the door's open and I heard this sort of growling."

He paused as if uncertain how to go on.

"Growling?" Galbraith prompted.

"It was a really angry noise, not like something you'd expect to hear from a dog."

"Do you get many dogs round here?"

"Not really. They don't allow pets."

"So tell me about this dog."

"It was big. Really big. Grey with shaggy hair. I didn't take much of a look, to be honest. I was trying to get my keys out as quickly as I could. It scared me."

"Did it actually attack you?"

"That was what was strange. He stepped forward and opened its mouth. I could see its teeth. They seemed…" He paused again. He looked pale, Galbraith thought, as if even the memory of the animal disturbed him. This time Galbraith did not prompt and, after a moment, Alex continued. "They seemed unusually long. Like fangs really."

He was white as a sheet, thought Galbraith.

"Finnis, can you get him a glass of water?"

He waited while Finnis went to the kitchen. There was the sound of a tap running and then she returned with the water.

Alex raised it to his lips with a trembling hand and took a long, slow sip.

"I was very shaken up. I may have imagined the next bit."

"I'd like you to describe it anyway."

Another drink.

"It seemed to rear up on its hind legs. Its face was level with mine. I was shaking. I dropped my keys. I was locked out with this thing facing me. I thought it was going to kill me."

"But it didn't."

"No. It suddenly stopped and sniffed. Then it shook its head. Its jaws were still open and it was growling. When it shook its head spittle hit me on the face. I tried to scream but I couldn't. I froze. Then it dropped back to the ground and ran off."

"Where did it go?"

"I saw it head round the corner and I grabbed up my keys and got inside. I didn't hang about to see what happened to it after that."

"And did you tell anybody about it?"

"No." Alex shook his head. "I just wanted to forget about it. It was scary but I thought I was imagining it as more of a thing than it really was. I mean, in the end it was only a dog."

Galbraith hurried to agree with him. It was only a dog but, as Alex had recognised, a dangerous one. "We've had reports of a dangerous dog in the area. We're going to try to track it down before it injures anyone."

"Well I'm glad you're taking it seriously. But there seem to be a lot of police for one dog."

Galbraith nodded. "We have to take these things seriously, sir. And it is a very big dog."

He headed back to the lift with Constable Finnis.

"I didn't realise we'd been called out because of a dog, sir."

"But you brought it straight to me."

"'Anything unusual,' I was told, sir."

Galbraith decided he liked Finnis.

"Sometimes we start with an accidental death and a senior officer evaluates the situation and decides it should be a murder enquiry. Other times we start with a murder enquiry and a senior officer…" He paused and gave her a meaningful look. "That would be me."

She nodded.

"The senior officer decides we're looking for a big dog. Which is what tomorrow's newspapers will say." He gave her another look. "I hope you're on board with that, constable."

Finnis nodded again.

"A big dog, sir. Sergeant must have mentioned it in his brief. I should have been paying more attention."

* * *

The good news, Pole and Galbraith were both agreed, was that they could now warn people to be on the alert. Extra police patrols were not only acceptable to local residents but positively demanded.

The bad news was that they knew that the creature they were hunting was targeting its attacks.

"But how," Galbraith asked, "could it tell that the first man wasn't one of the kind of residents he was after?"

"I imagine that werewolves share with their canine cousins a pronounced sense of smell. And the odour of a man who showers daily before applying the male fragrance of the moment is likely to differ from that of the long-term unemployed. Have you identified the victim by the way?"

"Joseph McCann. Easy to identify as he's known to the local police. He lives in one of the remaining council flats in the block where he regularly beats up his wife, who always insists that her bruises were caused when she tripped into a door. He has three children and basically survives on the money that is supposed to be spent on their food. Social workers keep threatening to start care proceedings but money's tight and…" He trailed off, shrugging helplessly.

"Well at least Mr McCann will not be missed."

"Strangely enough, I'm told his wife is distraught. I'll never understand women."

"I doubt I'll ever truly understand Mortals."

They sat in Pole's apartment but, for once, they were not enjoying his whisky. Galbraith had decided it was time for him to make a contribution and he had turned up bearing a six pack of craft ales. Pole, it turned out, owned no beer glasses, but his whisky tumblers were generously sized and they were drinking from those. Pole was doing his very best to appreciate his gift, but

Galbraith wondered if he had made a mistake. If he was being perfectly honest, the beers that had tasted more than acceptable at home seemed to lack something here.

Galbraith tried to sum up the situation as he would if he were leading a regular team in his own police station.

"We know that our man is around six feet tall and slim built. We have one suit of clothing that he appears to have worn only once and that briefly. A thorough search in the area of Inkster House hasn't found any clothing this time. Either our man has realised that he can't get back to the clothes he has stashed away or he has managed to switch back and left wearing them."

"Or we haven't searched far enough away. Werewolves can cover ground very quickly."

"We have to be realistic. Checking every bush and shrub takes time. People go on about how wonderful it is that there is so much green space around London. It's a lot less wonderful when you are searching it. These estates are full of patches of grass with shrubs all over them. And there are hedges. And playing fields and local parks. The estate is in an area bounded by the mainline railways into London and the A3205, which is a big road, mainly dual carriageway. We're working on the basis that those are boundaries he would try to avoid in wolf form."

"I understand the reality of the constraints you operate under." Pole's tone was carefully neutral and Galbraith suspected he didn't understand the constraints at all. "But we are talking about a creature that we believe has travelled from Vauxhall to Richmond without any reported sightings. I think it's probably capable of crossing a road."

Galbraith rested his face on his hand. Pole was right, of course, but his being right wasn't helping. "So what would you do?"

"I'd ask myself where he could change out of his clothes and take on his wolf shape – a process which is far from instantaneous – with a reasonable chance of not being seen. That rules out the sort of shrubbery that is planted around a space of common ground. Playing fields are no use either because they are flat and provide no proper cover."

Pole went to a bookcase and took down a large A-Z of London. Galbraith realised that, since Google maps had become ubiquitous on people's phones, he had hardly seen any A-Zs – and even before that, he had never seen one bound in leather.

Pole noticed the expression on his face. “Look around you, Chief Inspector. If you lived here, wouldn’t you want to disguise the somewhat garish cover of the London street plan?”

Galbraith doubted that he would go to the trouble and expense of having a map book rebound but, then again, he wouldn’t have an A-Z in the first place.

Pole had opened the book at the pages that included Inkster House. He pointed at areas of greenery to the east and west. “I’d consider the possibilities of York Gardens and Shillington Gardens.”

“Both in our search area.”

“True. But here...” He traced his finger south. “We have Clapham Common. There is quite a lot of cover from trees and scrub.”

“Across the busiest set of railway lines in the country.”

“In the dark. It’s surprisingly difficult to spot things in the dark when you are inside a lighted carriage. And I think the presence of the railway line was part of his plan. If he failed to change back, he would follow the railway back to Richmond.”

Galbraith shrugged reluctant agreement. “But even if you are right, I can’t search the whole of Clapham Common. It’s too big and, as you said, there are too many places a bag could be hidden.”

“But now that we are publicly looking for a dangerous dog, we can at least send officers to patrol the place. They can keep their eyes open and talk to people about anything unusual they might have seen.”

Both men drained their glasses in tacit agreement.

“An interesting experiment,” Pole said, smacking his lips with an expression of intense concentration. “But I believe there is such a thing as a whisky chaser.”

Galbraith admitted that he had heard the term. Pole got the bottle.

* * *

The hunt for a dangerous dog had seized the imagination of the press on what turned out to have been a quiet news day. Pole had expressed alarm that one of the tabloids had headlined its story ‘Hunt for London Werewolf’, but Galbraith reassured him that it was unlikely that readers would treat this as anything other than journalistic hyperbole.

The 'dangerous dog' story meant that they were able to involve more officers in the hunt, even if many of them were just asked to report on things that came up in their daily contact with the public. This was, as Pole had suggested, especially the case for police patrolling round Clapham Common, with extra officers patrolling the Common itself.

Galbraith's office now resembled a miniature Incident Room, with files filling with intelligence from police stations all over south-west London. Most of it, he suspected, was useless. Some was useful, but irrelevant. Dog theft was a big problem in London and the sudden police interest in reports of animals barking late at night meant knocks on the doors of several crooks with sheds housing distressed pooches. The owners were delighted to get them back but it moved Galbraith no nearer to finding the werewolf.

There were a couple of interesting reports from Clapham Common. One was that somebody reported seeing a naked man on the Common the evening of the latest killing. Some recent attacks in the area had driven most of the dubious men who used to hang around there to seek alternative places to prowl and, in any case, it was a bit late in the year for even the most enthusiastic exhibitionist to strip off all their clothes. Galbraith put that report in the very slim file he was using to store promising leads.

The other thing to catch his attention was the report of a break-in at the football changing rooms. It was put down to vandalism or a couple looking for a sheltered spot for some illicit lovemaking, but the local station had duly copied the report to Galbraith who was struck by two things about it. Firstly, it was on the evening of the murder and, secondly, it was very close to the spot at which the naked man had been reported.

When he told Pole, the man from Section S agreed that it was worth investigating. "I'll meet you there this evening at about 6.30. That's around the time that the man was reported. It makes sense to visit the scene at the same time."

Galbraith tactfully refrained from pointing out that it also meant that Pole would not need to leave his home until almost dark. He didn't like to be reminded of the limitations his lifestyle imposed on him.

Galbraith arrived first. The sun was already below the trees when Pole emerged from the shadows, his hat pulled down shading his eyes and a scarf swaddling his face. Given the chill of the evening, he blended in with the few others in the park.

The lock had been repaired, but Galbraith had been given a key and the two detectives let themselves in.

"It's a shame I only heard about this today." It was a Saturday and the hut had been used by several teams playing five-a-side that afternoon. "I doubt there'll be much sign of him – assuming it was him."

"How did he get in?"

"Jemmied the lock. Probably with a screwdriver judging from the marks, according to the local CID."

"Nothing taken?"

"Nothing taken and, apart from the lock, nothing damaged."

They looked round the place: a single bare room with benches along one wall and pegs for hanging clothes. Another door led through to some toilets.

"There does not appear to be much that could be damaged," said Pole.

"True. But when you get vandals breaking in there's usually graffiti, maybe a smashed window. Sometimes they break the toilets, just for fun. This time there was nothing, so it looks like whoever it was may simply have been seeking shelter."

"Were there any used prophylactics found?"

Galbraith hesitated. It was a while since he had come across that word. "No, the CID did not report any condoms. That doesn't prove it wasn't a couple though. She might have been on the pill."

"Or he might have been careless," conceded Pole. He was prowling around the room and Galbraith imagined him sniffing at the walls. Then he knelt on the floor. There was no doubt about it. He was sniffing.

"Anything?"

"It was too long ago and there have been too many people here since, but there is the faintest whiff of something not quite right. I think we should work on the assumption that our friend might have been here."

It was not much to go on but it was, in Pole's opinion, enough for Section S to organise a search of the area. "Frankly," he said, "I'd rather use regular police and keep our existence well into the background, but it's going to be difficult to justify a fingertip search without awkward questions being raised."

The search started that night. Generators chugged away powering arc lights as the Section S searchers worked their way out from the changing rooms. Technicians swept the ground with what looked like metal detectors, only Pole assured Galbraith that they weren't and when Galbraith asked what they were, Pole said that they were special equipment and that it was best just left at that.

They carried on in daylight the next morning, but by noon they admitted there was nothing there to find.

Galbraith told Pole over the phone. As soon as dawn had begun to glimmer in the sky, he had made his excuses and headed home.

"It's disappointing, but we can always review the CCTV of the area. It's tedious but often productive."

Sometimes, Galbraith thought, Pole's ignorance of the practicalities of 21st century policing could be very irritating. "I know the papers are always saying CCTV is everywhere, but there's not a lot on Clapham Common. When people are told that their every move is being watched, what nobody says is that it is generally being watched by a privately owned CCTV system that we have no access to. Round Clapham Common, most of them will be cameras set up by local residents to cover their front doors. OK, they usually give us a bit of the pavement as well, but it's not as if we can visit every household and ask to review their doorbell camera footage."

Galbraith heard Pole chuckle on his phone. "You forget that Section S has powers that we don't admit to the regular police. Most of those private CCTV cameras connect to the Internet and we have, as you might say, very good connections of our own. We are linked in to all those cameras – so, in a manner of speaking, the conspiracy theorists are right: your every move can be watched. Not," he added hastily, "that we make a habit of it. But in this case, we can review the footage from last Thursday night and we shall see what comes up."

"And you think we'll spot him?"

"I hope so. Otherwise our best hope is to wait for another body."

"Charming," said Galbraith.

"Realistic," said Pole. "After the first couple of hundred years you have few comforting illusions left."

CHAPTER 11: In which Garold takes a train

It had worked!

OK, there were glitches, things that still needed to be ironed out, but it had worked.

He had travelled from Clapham Common to Inkster House without any excitement. The idea of crossing the railway lines at Clapham Junction had worried him, but once in wolf form he was able to run across without breaking stride.

The only problem once he arrived was that he had been about to attack that silly little man who dropped his keys, when he realised that this wasn't some hopeless drop-out from decent society at all. He smelled far too clean.

It was interesting, Garold thought, that it was the smell he had responded to. As a human, he would have noticed that the man's clothes were just too smart, his grooming too perfect. These things hardly registered with the wolf, though. For him, it was all about the smell.

Even when he realised a mistake had been made, it was a struggle to stop himself from tearing the man's throat open. Wolves, he thought, were not big on self-restraint once their blood was up. The human bit of his brain had struggled with the animal's baser instincts – and triumphed. He was a man: if he believed, he could do anything! It was a good thing, though, that that other wretch had turned up so soon afterwards. Then he had been able to relax and allow himself to feed.

Afterwards he had left the body in the dumpster. It was a nice touch, that: a sort of calling card. After that, he had returned to Clapham Common and hidden away in the changing rooms, waiting for the clonazepam to kick in. As he expected, it took rather longer than the 30 minutes that the doctor had told him, but that wasn't a problem. After three quarters of an hour he felt himself relaxing. As he calmed, the claws grew shorter, the body hair was absorbed back into his skin and his jaw reshaped, losing the pointed muzzle of a wolf and turning back to the dull conformity of a human face.

The change, with the movements of bone and skeletal musculature, was inevitably painful – not a problem when he moved from human to wolf because wolves have quite a high pain threshold. It was, though, a very unpleasant experience when the change was in the other direction. To his relief, he discovered that the clonazepam reduced his sensitivity to pain – an unexpected, but wholly welcome, side-effect.

He retrieved the clothes from the sports bag he had left in the changing room and dressed himself. It was only then that he realised that clonazepam was not, perhaps, the idea solution to his problems. The drug was making him overwhelmingly drowsy. It was all he could do to stop himself from lying down on the bench and allowing himself to sleep. He thought of the headlines: 'Tory MP found 'tired and emotional' on Clapham Common.' That would not be a good look for a man who still had political ambitions.

He forced himself to get up and staggered out of the hut. He was all too aware that he was giving a very good impression of a drunk, but, luckily, there was nobody there to see it.

There was no question of his getting to Richmond. He was in no state to walk and even hailing a taxi could lead to his being recognised and nobody was safe from scandal in this age of camera phones and social media. Fortunately, there are trains running all night from Clapham Junction to Victoria, so he could at least get within walking distance of his office in Portcullis House. He thought he would be able to manage the last mile providing that he took it slowly.

In the end, it took almost an hour to make that walk. He decided to avoid Victoria Street – too many people and too many CCTV cameras. He moved instead through side streets. He might have been in human form, but there was part of his brain where the wolf was still struggling to maintain its hold and this part guided him instinctively into the shadows, gliding through the darkness like the creature of the night that it still was. That close to Parliament there were inevitably police patrols but most passed him without noticing and the few he did saw only a man perhaps a little the worse for wear, but nothing requiring their attention.

He could hardly avoid being seen by the security guard on the desk at Portcullis House but Commons staff are encouraged to exercise a certain amount of discretion. Garold was not the first to be seen the worse for drink and the guard studiously avoided any comment as Garold clutched at his desk for support before braving the last few yards across the lobby to the lifts.

* * *

Fridays, when the House is sitting at all on a Friday, are generally quiet. It's a day for private members bills and bits of Parliamentary business that are not particularly interesting. It allows members to get away early, ready to spend the weekend opening fetes and caballing with their constituency committees.

This Friday, there was a motion about the effect of over-fishing on the marine environment. It was the sort of thing that exercised environmentalists but rather irritated the government. Garold had intended to speak in the debate, environmentalists being an important part of his electoral base. The whips, whose job it was to discourage anything that irritated the government, would just as soon see him take a duvet day and pass on the debate which, thanks to the clonazepam, was exactly what he did.

'OK,' he thought when he woke up, sometime around three in the afternoon, 'it's annoyed some of my local tree-huggers, but how many of them will have noticed a speech on Friday morning? It's not as if it would even make the TV news. The whips, on the other hand, will see it as a sign of my loyalty and reliability. I'll tell them that I changed my mind when I realised that it could really embarrass the government. Probably best not mention that I was out of my head on drugs at the time.'

So, on balance he felt his efforts had been a success. His approach needed finessing for the future, though. He couldn't risk more journeys like the one he had taken last night and he could not rely on nobody noticing his absence the following morning.

The problem was that clonazepam was not the ideal drug for him. Much better was triazolam – a drug very similar to clonazepam but one that clears your system much faster. The problem with triazolam was that, while it could be legally prescribed in the USA, it was banned in the UK.

Of course, the fact that it was banned didn't mean that you couldn't obtain it. Garold had visited enough drop-in centres catering for troubled young people for him to have a reasonable working knowledge of the London drug scene. Uppers and downers were common enough and he was confident he knew people who knew people who could get hold of what he needed.

That would help making a smoother, faster transition from wolf to functioning human, but what about the other way? He had, it's true, managed to transform, even though the moon was six days past the full. But it had been a struggle and the time of the change, when he was neither fully human nor fully werewolf, was a period of extreme vulnerability. He needed to make that period shorter and he didn't want to have to wait until only days off the full moon before he could repeat the experiment.

The answer, it seemed to him, was more drugs. The kids always talked about "uppers and downers" as if they were naturally taken together. And why not? If the downers calmed him enough to change back to a man, then would the uppers not facilitate the change from man to wolf? And if the moonlight was crucial, could he not simulate this with special electric lighting?

Another hour or so with Google and he had the answer. The drug that should increase his rage to levels that might transform him into a ravening wolf was a methamphetamine sold as Desoxyn in the United States. As to the lighting: there were several companies who would set up lamps to mimic moonlight.

* * *

Strangely enough, it proved much easier to find someone who would supply the methamphetamine than to get the artificial moonlight installed.

At first Garold had been unhappy with the idea of buying crack cocaine through his youthful middlemen. A seventeen-year-old with chemistry A levels had had to spend a while explaining that while Desoxyn came in a neat little tub and crack cocaine arrived in tiny ziplock bags, the active ingredients were more or less the same. The 'more or less' worried him at first, but then he reflected that it was hardly as if he was planning to take Desoxyn the way the label said it was supposed to be used, so wouldn't 'more or less' be good enough?

Three hours after taking this decision, Garold was the happy owner of 100 grams of crystal meth and fifty little blue pills stamped with triazolam's US brand name, Halcion.

It took rather longer, though, for him to arrange the other elements of his plan.

If he was to use lamps to mimic the effect of moonlight, he needed a base outside Portcullis House. He could set up the lighting he needed but then, already in wolf form, he would have to leave the building to make his kills and, though the staff were good at turning a blind eye to peculiar behaviour from MPs, the sight of a wolf strolling through the corridors of power would, he thought, be too much for them to ignore. First, then, he had to get a flat near the House. Although a taxi to his Richmond constituency would take him only an hour or so, he would not be alone in keeping a flat near Westminster. It was convenient, other members had assured him, not just to have somewhere to rest during late-night sittings, although nowadays they were rare, but (and at this point most would tap their noses or wink conspiratorially) it meant you could have a place to work late with your (invariably young, usually female) researchers.

There's a surprising amount of greenery in Pimlico, which means that if you have a ground floor flat and can slip quietly into the night then, if you have the speed and agility of a werewolf, you can travel a surprisingly long way without drawing attention. It's also handy for Victoria station and Garold already knew how easy it was to travel unseen along the railway lines.

A lot of MPs live in Dolphin Square, but it's not that easy to slip in or out unnoticed. There are other squares nearby that suited his needs, though.

For most people, renting a ground floor flat in St George's Square would be almost impossible, but the combination of Garold's status as an MP and the money he had inherited from his family meant that he had accomplished the near impossible in less than a week.

It took a further three days, though, to persuade a company to install moonlight lamps in the flat. In the end he found a firm called 'Serene Selene'. "We're named after the Greek goddess of the moon," a rather Sloane-y voice had explained on the phone. "We're really all about recreating the moonlight ambiance in gardens or large conservatories." The tone clearly implied that she was thinking of the sort of conservatory you found in Kew Gardens, rather than a glass extension to your terraced house.

Garold pointed out that it was November and a moonlit romantic ambience did not combine well with hypothermia. "I work strange hours in the House and you must appreciate that it's stressful. I'm not looking for romance, but I do find moonlight relaxing and I'd like to have that effect when I get here away from my office."

"It won't really be a moonlight *experience*," she said. Somehow she made the word 'experience' sound sexual.

"I don't need the experience," Garold explained. "Just that delicious blue light."

It took a while, but Serene Selene eventually agreed to send what they insisted on calling a 'moon ambience technician' to St George's Square where, after much fussing with light meters and tape measures, he installed two lights in the flat's tiny study. (Garold had money, but there was a limit to the size of house even he could afford in that postcode.) More light readings and adjustment of reflectors and filters resulted in an assurance that his flat would now have the visual quality of a moonlit glade – if that glade featured Amara furniture and a remarkable lack of foliage.

Garold couldn't help feeling that, in the end, he was simply buying two very expensive lightbulbs. No matter: when he turned them on that evening, the effect was convincing. Even without drugs, even without anger, he could feel the hairs rising on his arms and a sort of preparatory twitching in his limbs.

It was time.

CHAPTER 12: In which our heroes watch TV

Galbraith had spent days reviewing CCTV. While it was true that there was little in the way of CCTV coverage of Clapham Common, it now seemed fairly certain that the creature they were after must have crossed the railway, probably around Clapham Junction. Unlike the Common, Clapham Junction is very well-covered by CCTV. Trespassers are taken seriously: one child playing chicken can bring much of London's rail network to a halt round there and Counter Terrorism (the 'real' Counter Terrorism, as Galbraith thought of it, as opposed to Pole's dubious colleagues) kept a close eye on it too.

There was *something* – a blur moving fast across the lines. Maybe a fox; maybe a dog; maybe their man. But it moved fast, it kept low. It was impossible to be sure.

There were one or two other shadows on the residential streets – slipping in and out of gardens, ducking through parks. But, Galbraith asked himself, isn't that what foxes do?

As evening fell, he was surprised to get a visit from Pole.

"I thought I'd have a look at the CCTV you've got. I'm hardly set up for viewing at my apartment."

That, Galbraith thought, was certainly true. He knew Pole had a computer, but he avoided doing anything as vulgar as looking at it.

He gestured at the guest chair and Pole pulled it closer to the screen.

"I've had no joy so far."

Pole looked at the blurry images and the time clock in the corner.

"You're tracking him from the Common to the kill?"

"Trying to. I think I can see him, but it's impossible to be sure."

"What about on the way back?"

"On the way out we have a starting point and an end point and we know when he was there to threaten our owner-occupier. But we don't know exactly when he left or if he went straight back to the Common – that's if he went back to the Common at all."

"We're almost certain he was in the changing hut and we haven't found any clothes. It stands to reason that he went back."

"Or he abandoned them and some tramp took them. Or he came back the next day. Even if he returned that night, it's too wide a time frame. We can't go through hours of CCTV just to say we think we saw something vaguely wolf-like at, say, half an hour after midnight. Even if we did, it moves us no further forward."

"What if we were looking for a man?"

"Life would be a lot easier. But we're looking for a wolf."

"A wolf who, if our theory about the clothes is correct, changes back into a man in the course of the night."

"There's no CCTV on the hut and once he – it – has changed back into human form we have no idea who we are looking for."

"Why not see if there were any people behaving strangely in the area that night?"

"Strangely?"

"He's been hunting through the streets of London as a wolf. Then he's changed back to being a man which, I imagine, takes it out of you. Now he's walking the streets in a cheap suit in the middle of the night. Don't you think he might stand out a little?"

Galbraith put his palms down on his desk in a gesture that mingled irritation and resignation. He really should have thought of that himself. It was bad enough that Pole was always ahead of him when it came to his understanding of the supernatural without him pointing out something that a human policeman should have worked out without help.

"I'll get another viewer. We can split them between us."

"We only want to see the film from the cameras nearest to the park. We need a sort of virtual cordon. If we see anyone of interest, we can focus on the cameras that let us track them on their way."

Galbraith nodded. It made sense.

"Don't blame yourself, Chief Inspector." Pole's tone was placatory. "You've been working on this all day, whereas I come fresh from a good rest."

True enough, Galbraith thought. And one advantage of his unconventional partner was that between the two of them they could keep checking the CCTV 24 hours a day.

Ten minutes later they sat down with a screen apiece. It was going to be a long night.

* * *

There were, in Galbraith's view, a ridiculous number of people wandering around Clapham of an evening. Many of them were wearing suits – late home from the office, hurrying back to settle in front of the TV with a cold drink. Some of them looked as if they may have had several drinks already.

They agreed to concentrate on anyone carrying a sports bag. No bag had been found, despite the best efforts of Section S, so it seemed likely that he was still carrying it. Anyone with a suit but no bag was worth a look, in case it had been discarded somewhere Section S had missed, but men with briefcases could be safely ignored.

They tracked several men who wove unsteadily along pavements before vanishing into the bushes, only to emerge a minute or two later with disarranged clothing and, in a couple of cases, suspicious damp patches on their trousers that suggested drunken urination rather than anything supernatural.

One respectable-looking, and apparently sober fellow vanished into the bushes for rather longer. They were about to start searching for any cameras that might have recorded him coming out when Galbraith caught a glimpse of him hiding in the undergrowth, staring at the houses opposite.

"Looks like a Peeping Tom or a jealous lover. Either way I'll pass it over to uniforms to make a few calls."

It was another half hour before he saw something that might have been a fox or there again…

"What do you think?" he asked Pole.

"It's possible. Let's move on ten minutes and see if we turn anybody up after that."

Ten minutes after the 'might have been a fox', the streets seemed unusually deserted. It was getting later and the few figures that wandered round Clapham were more casually dressed.

"There." Pole pointed. It was a man in a suit, staggering as if drunk. He was carrying a sports bag but as they watched he dropped it into someone's rubbish bin put out for collection.

"So much for the bag," said Galbraith. "It looks like our man though." The problem was that he walked with the posture of the very drunk, head down as if looking to see where he was placing his feet. "I can't even tell how tall he is, let alone get a decent view of his face. He could well be about six foot though, couldn't he?"

Pole nodded and they watched as the figure swayed beyond the camera, heading north.

Galbraith pointed to a map on the desk beside his monitor. "Here are the nearest cameras in that direction. We'll follow him until he takes us home."

They followed him towards the station. Tracking people by CCTV, even with all the advantages that Section S's technology gave them, isn't as easy as they make it seem on the television. Many of the images are blurred and grainy and sometimes they were not absolutely sure they were following right man. Even in London there are many streets which do not feature on the feed from any cameras and many of the cameras covering likely spots turn out not to work properly.

After a while they were sure that he was walking towards Clapham Junction so they skipped to the camera focused on the station entrance. Sure enough it picked up the staggering figure in the cheap suit. Still, though, he had his head down.

"We can add brown hair to the description, but not much else."

The figure moved towards the ticket barrier.

"We'll get him when he taps in. We've got the time and the machine he uses. We can trace the card."

They saw him stop and tap his hands against his jacket pockets. Galbraith recognised that gesture. "He didn't leave his cards in the suit. That must have seemed a wise precaution at the time but…"

They watched as someone else approached the barrier and, as they stepped through it, he followed immediately behind, miming tapping his ticket as he walked through.

Galbraith gave a look of disgust. "Great."

"Well," said Pole, "if we can't get him for murder, there's always fare dodging."

"Very droll." Galbraith switched to the feed from the next camera and the image on the screen gave way to static. The CCTV at stations was not nearly as reliable as Network Rail liked to claim it was. He switched to the next camera.

That didn't work either, or the next.

Galbraith swore. "He's got the luck of the devil."

"Quite possibly literally," said Pole.

Galbraith ignored him, switching from camera to camera with an alacrity that would have amazed Sgt Green, who was convinced that Galbraith was far too much of a dinosaur to master new technology. Finally they came on one that worked. The two of them watched it for the ten minutes after their suspect had vanished from view.

"Nothing!" Galbraith slammed his fist on the desk in an unusual display of irritation. "We've lost him."

"We know he went on one of the first six platforms. None of them lead out towards Richmond. If he wasn't going that way, it's reasonable to assume he's heading back towards the location of the later kills and that would mean Victoria. Take a look at what you can find there."

Even late in the evening, there are a lot of people getting off trains into Victoria. Many are wearing suits. Quite a lot seem the worse for drink. The two detectives spent an hour watching the CCTV feeds and did their best to follow a couple of possible leads out of the station, but it was impossible.

"We were so bloody close."

"We're wiser than we were," said Pole. "Added to about six feet tall and slim, we have brown hair and now based in central London. It's more than we knew before. And he's getting careless. We'll get him next time."

* * *

More than a week had passed since the last killing and with no moon at all for the next few nights, Galbraith and Pole were both turning their attention to other things. Galbraith had decided that if he was going to be tied down with administration, it might as well be something useful. After his experience with the cameras at Clapham he persuaded his superintendent that he should conduct a review of CCTV coverage in their police district and make some calls on the owners of sites where cameras were regularly out of action. He was coming to accept the idea that his days in front-line policing were numbered and this seemed a useful way to ease himself into an administrative role.

Pole, too, he imagined must be doing whatever he did between investigations. There couldn't, Galbraith thought, be enough criminal acts by supernatural beings to keep him employed full-time. He wondered about Pole's occasional hints about the security services. Perhaps in between solving the odd murder, he was exsanguinating enemies of the state, trapped by a promise to a long-dead monarch. It didn't, Galbraith decided, bear thinking about, so he took care not to think about it.

Galbraith was still enjoying the regular hours that came with an administrative role. Turn off the computer, lock the office door and home in time for a microwave meal and a glass of beer in front of the TV. He liked detective stories: the neat orderliness of them – a wonderful antidote to the tensions he often felt after a day of real-life policing.

He was often in bed by ten. After years of irregular hours he appreciated a good night's sleep.

Just before 1.30 he dreamt he was in the Scottish play and the bell was ringing. Macbeth was saying, "Hear it not Galbraith, for it is the knell that summons thee…"

That was no castle bell: that was the phone. Galbraith forced himself awake. It was Pole. "There's been another one," he said.

CHAPTER 13: In which Garold returns to Pimlico

He would return to Pimlico, he decided. He had to make the change at home where the lights were installed and travelling across the bridges in wolf form was unrealistic: there was too much risk of being seen. So it must be north of the river and he wanted to make it reasonably close so he could be sure of getting there, making his kill and returning safely before the triazolam kicked in.

Pimlico was fine. It's what is euphemistically referred to as a 'mixed' area, which means that the very rich live only streets away from those who struggle to survive on benefit.

The biggest estate in Pimlico is the Churchill Estate, built after the war on an area near the river that had suffered more than its share of bomb damage. It was once a model for the social housing of the future but by now parts of it were near-derelict and some were being demolished for redevelopment.

He would have to be careful, he knew. There were decent people living there – honest people who worked hard and did their best and paid their taxes. The sort of people that he stuck up for in his constituency. But this wasn't Richmond East: this was the inner-city and there were too many of the feckless poor – the immigrants, the lazy, the drug addled. He had been to so many meetings where his fellow MPs talked about schemes for cleansing London of poverty and crime, but nothing had come of it. Now he had the power: now, at last, some actual, real, cleansing could start.

It had been a late night at the House. They had been sitting until ten and then he wanted to have a word with one of the junior ministers for the environment. On his way out, he had been waylaid by Marianne, a petite woman who wore her years well. Usually Garold would have been tempted to offer her a drink anyway, because she was always fun to be with. Tonight he had plans in which a drink with Marianne didn't feature, but when she suggested they go to the bar, he had little choice but to agree – because Marianne was a whip.

Garold remembered how, before he was elected, he always thought that the whips must be fearsome individuals who could make strong men weep and bully anyone into unquestioning support of their party line. And, indeed, some whips were exactly like that. But there are many whips and each plays to their strengths. Marianne's strength was a flirtatious charm.

Garold didn't know why he was being singled out for Marianne's attention. The government's majority was thin, but he had taken care to be on his best behaviour lately. He found that the thrill of teasing the whips with his environmentalist views palled compared to the excitement he was getting from his nocturnal adventures.

Marianne bought the drinks – an espresso martini for him and something complicated and non-alcoholic for her – and settled down at a quiet table. She was smiling, so Garold reckoned he couldn't be in any trouble, but he was still surprised when, after the bare minimum of social chat about his constituency and his environmental issues, she came to the point of their drinks.

"I'm just checking that you are really happy with the way the Government has been handling …" She made a vague stirring gesture with her hand, almost spilling her drink. "… things."

It was a tricky question. "Things" (they changed every week, but never in a good way) weren't going well and even the most junior backbencher would have to be having doubts about the way Government ministers were dealing with them. Obviously it would never do to tell one of the whips – even Marianne, with her cheerful smile and her bouncy manner – that you thought the Cabinet was a choice bunch of idiots and the PM was losing control. At the same time, an excessive avowal of loyalty would suggest a level of political naivety that could rule out political advancement.

He sipped his martini and put on what he liked to think of as his 'concerned face' – one that he used a lot when listening to constituents' tales of woe. "Well, Marianne, these are difficult times and, inevitably there has been the odd misstep. But overall I think we're doing pretty well. It's particularly difficult to steer a steady course when our majority is so slender, but the PM is holding up better than the press gives him credit for."

He knew he had judged it just right when he saw a smile grow even wider. "And we can rely on you, can't we, Christopher? You're happy to throw your weight behind the PM?"

"Of course, Marianne. I know I've not always seen eye to eye with the government on environmental issues, but I've never defied the whip."

"I know, Christopher. And I just want to tell you that the whips know. You'll have heard rumours of a reshuffle?"

He had, of course, but until this minute he had not known whether to take them seriously.

"Make sure you leave your phone switched on." She smiled at him again. "Keep the faith," she said and gulped down her non-alcoholic cocktail.

"It's been good to talk," she said and glanced theatrically at her watch. "But I must run. Enjoy your drink."

She dashed off, waving. He sat, sipping at his martini and thinking over what Marianne had said. He had no intention of doing anything that might annoy the party. Once, perhaps, he would have risked some minor rebellion to demonstrate to himself and his voters that he was a free spirit who could think for himself. But now that seemed a foolish self-indulgence. He would toe the line. He was a coming man.

Meanwhile, he had his new project – something the whips would never learn about. Perhaps, if he was made a junior minister, he might be able to make some changes here and there. Until then, though, he was going to hit the streets. There, he was really going to make a difference.

* * *

It was almost midnight by the time he got home. He wondered if it might not be more sensible to rest tonight and hunt tomorrow but he knew he would be too excited to sleep if he went to bed. He had made all his plans. He wouldn't put off now.

He slid the window open, closed the curtains, stripped off his clothes and turned on the artificial moonlight. Then he took a small crystal of crack from the ziplock bag his dealer had sold him and put it on some tin foil to heat it. He had toyed with the idea of a pipe. A crack pipe had seemed somehow cooler than messing about with kitchen foil, but at the same time he thought the idea of owning what court reports referred to as "drug paraphernalia" identified him with the crackheads he so despised. His use of cocaine was, after all, entirely utilitarian. He wasn't taking drugs for fun. He didn't need the buzz of illicit chemicals when there were throats to tear open. No crack would ever match the thrill of blood.

The crystal was bubbling gently in the heat from a scented candle. (He had no intention of using a disposable lighter and adding to the world's supply of plastic waste.) He put a straw up his nose (paper, of course) and inhaled.

The effect was almost immediate. He felt his pulse race and then a wave of emotion brought the beginning of the change. His bones cracked and regrew, his jaws stretched into a muzzle. He felt the power. The world was brighter and full of scents. The perfumed candle was cloying. He had to get out – out into the fresh air or, at least, air as fresh as was available in the centre of London.

The human side of his brain barely had time to take the Desoxyn before he was racing through the shadows towards Churchill Gardens.

There are few gardens, as such, on the estate, but there are bushes and hedges and places a hunter can lie in wait for his prey. So Garold waited.

He had done a lot of research before choosing this location. He had spent some time in the Commons library looking benefit levels around London. His own constituency, he was pleased to see, had fewer people on benefit than almost anywhere in London, but Westminster ranked around halfway down. It certainly had more than its share of people that liberals thought of as "disadvantaged" but whom he preferred to view as feckless and lazy. Most of them lived in the north of the borough, too far for him to travel safely, but there would be enough in Churchill Gardens for him to be able to find a suitable victim.

The estate didn't feature the sort of landmark tower blocks that had marked his previous kill zones. Some taller blocks were mixed in with maisonettes and terraces. It was, he thought, a good place to hunt, closer to the idea of hunting in open country than lurking around a tower block and waiting for a victim. He had learned from his mistake at Inkster House. He wouldn't leap out on the first person he saw. He had been saved at the last moment when he realised that the man he had attacked hadn't smelled right. His wolf-brain hadn't analysed the scent or considered the implications of hair shampoo and an up-market aftershave. It had just known. The human part of the creature he was when he was hunting had to learn to listen to the instincts of the wolf. Stay quiet and use your nose.

All those nights spent in Richmond Park when he was younger meant that he associated hunting with the smell of grass, the meaty odour of deer, odd aromas from the remains of picnics scattered here and there. It was London so, of course, there was always the background stench of petrol and diesel fumes, but the park was closed to traffic at night and the stink of the distant cars was easily ignored.

Here in the centre of town the smells were almost overwhelming. There was traffic: even at night the nearby main road along the Thames was always busy, but there were cars on the estate too. What were these people doing, coming and going at this hour of night, he wondered? And why did they have such disgusting diets: the stench of abandoned cartons with the discarded remains of fast-food was even more nauseating than the traffic fumes. The breeze from the Thames wafted the faint but (to a wolf) unmistakeable whiff of sewage into the streets where he was hunting. Overflowing bins carried a welter of smells, very few of them pleasant. There had been (he remembered the local MP complaining about it in the House) some sort of failure with the refuse collection, so many of the bins were piled high and the stench was revolting. Taking deep sniffs of the night air, analysing them for the undertones of poverty was not a good experience. Once or twice even the wolf nearly gagged and the human part of his brain was revolted. But soon enough there was a whiff of human that carried with it the smell of cigarettes and cider and despair. That would do.

He crouched beside one of the shrubs that an optimistic planner had scattered around the estate to give the impression of middle-class greenery. The effect was spoiled by the crisp packets caught among the leaves and the beer cans around the trunk, but as far as a werewolf was concerned the shrub was ideally suited for the hunt. He waited until he could hear the footsteps just a few metres away and then he pounced.

It was over quickly. It was the hunt that mattered – the hunt and the kill. He had no interest in celebrating the death. That was why he had left the corpses with the rubbish. The maisonettes in Churchill Gardens, though, had no convenient dumpsters. He realised he didn't care. He would leave the body where it lay. He had surely made his point.

He could still feel the crack cocaine coursing through his veins. He always felt more alive, his senses more vivid, when he was in wolf form. Now, though, the drugs had brought a new intensity to his experience. He wanted to kill again.

Back into the shadows, sniffing, waiting. Then springing out on his victim; the taste of blood – the warm, salt stickiness of it.

And back to St George's Square, quickly, before the Desoxyn kicked in.

Home. In through the window, silent in the darkness. Curled up safe in his own living room, already asleep as his body started to change.

CHAPTER 14: In which Galbraith also returns to Pimlico

"Another two, actually."

Once again, Galbraith was in a police car as Pole briefed him on the latest killings.

"There's little doubt that it's the same man, or whatever you want to call it. The victims lived on a council estate and have had their throats ripped out – but there are disturbing differences. Most obviously, this time there are two victims. Also, one of them wasn't unemployed. He worked on the bins for the council. He'd been working late, putting on extra shifts to clear the backlog here. He was just trying to get home.

It looks like two separate attacks, a quarter of a mile or so apart. The binman was the second to die. The first fitted the pattern: long-term unemployed. No tower block though. The bodies were left in the street, too – maybe because there weren't any convenient dumpsters where they were killed."

"It's in Pimlico, though, so not that far from the Abbots Estate killing."

"Indeed." Pole looked thoughtful. "It's the first time since he left Richmond Park that we've seen him strike in the same place twice. I can't help feeling that's significant."

"We think we tracked him to Victoria station after the last killing. So that's three times he's linked with this area."

"So…" Pole was oblivious of their surroundings. The car was pulling to a halt on Churchill Gardens Road, but Pole had his eyes closed. It seemed to Galbraith he was looking at a map in his head rather than the reality around them. "He starts in Richmond, then works his way towards the centre of town. Suppose he used to be based in Richmond, but now he lives somewhere near Victoria? Would that make sense?"

"We'd have to explain the trip out to Clapham."

"It's convenient by rail. He can kill in Clapham and be back to Victoria quickly."

"But why does this suddenly matter? He's not been worried about getting away quickly before."

Pole seemed to consider the question and then, with an apparent effort, pulled himself back into the present. "We'd better have a look at the bodies."

As he spoke, he was already opening the car door.

They walked towards the floodlights that had been set up at the murder scene. There was no ambulance this time. The body lay on a pavement covered by a white police forensic tent. As soon as they opened the flap and stepped in, they could see why an ambulance had not been called.

When the bodies had been left in dumpsters the extent of the damage had not been immediately apparent to the first people to find them. Here on the pavement, though, the ferocity of the attack was horribly obvious. Galbraith considered himself hardened to most forms of violent death but he recoiled from looking too closely at the bloody remains in the tent. Pole, though, squatted down to get a better view.

“The same sort of attack, but I would say more vicious than his earlier efforts. See here the bite has almost severed the neck.” He jiggled the head experimentally. “It's only held together by the spine.”

Galbraith reluctantly gave Pole's demonstration a glance before turning away.

“And there's more damage to the chest where the heart has been torn out.”

“Where are you going with this?”

Pole straightened and gave a half-shrug. “I'm not entirely sure. I'm just remarking that something has changed. There are two deaths; it's unusually violent, even for a werewolf attack; it's unusually close to a previous killing; and the bodies have simply been abandoned in the street. It's as if there is a sort of desperation to the whole thing.”

Galbraith grunted. He didn't concern himself overmuch with the mental state of supernatural monsters. That seemed more Pole's line of country and he was happy to leave it to him.

They walked around a corner and two hundred metres away there was another tent and another body. Galbraith glanced quickly at it, but Pole again gave it serious attention. “It's the same as the other.” He sighed. “I wish this wasn't quite so public. Bodies in the street are likely to draw attention and can't simply be written off as muggings. I'm afraid I'm going to have to work with my colleagues to handle the way this is presented. Gang killings, I think. There's been a lot in the press about young men carrying machetes. With any luck we can convince people that accounts for the wounds.”

“And our hapless council worker?”

"Wrong place, wrong time: a tragic reflection on the age we live in." He paused. "That may well be close to the truth actually."

"You don't think we'd be better going with the dangerous dog line then?"

"Do you think you could make that credible?" Pole waited and, when Galbraith did not reply, he nodded abruptly. "I didn't think so. Section S has some expertise in this area. I'll talk to my people and then we need to meet. We haven't even begun to discuss the most significant difference."

"Ah, yes." The first thing Galbraith had noticed was the absence of any moonlight at all, but the sight of the bodies and Pole's monologue on the clues these might or might not offer had put it out of his head.

"I think there may be some urgency in planning our next step," said Pole. "Do you think it would be possible to discuss it later tonight?"

'Later tonight,' Galbraith thought, meant tomorrow morning. At this time of year it would still be dark in the morning, so Pole would be happy being out and about. Blessing the fact that he had got to bed so early and thus had almost a whole four hours' sleep, he agreed. "It will have to be my office, though. I'm not hanging about on your doorstep waiting for you to get in."

"Of course, Chief Inspector: your office. Shall we say 5.00am?"

Galbraith nodded. If he was lucky, he might even get an hour or two's sleep at his desk.

* * *

In the end, Pole did not turn up until just before 6.00, allowing Galbraith nearly three hours of sleep. By the time he had drunk a cup of coffee, he felt almost wide awake. Pole, though, was looking rather the worse for wear. Covering up a very public double murder was apparently not as straightforward as he had hoped. "We should be alright now, though," he said. "So long as we don't have anybody who saw the whole thing and videoed it."

"I would have thought video might be rather useful."

"Hardly. We don't want people panicking about the werewolf and, in any case, we are reasonably confident we know what it looks like. If we see a werewolf, we have to contain it. We don't need to put it on an identity parade first. No, what we need is a photograph of the beast in human form, but we are getting there."

"Not fast enough." Galbraith gestured at a blurry still taken from the camera at Clapham junction.

"Six foot or thereabouts, slim build, Caucasian, brown hair. Plus, after last night, I'd say that he lives not that far from Victoria."

"It's still not enough," said Galbraith. "I think we need to get a move on. This started with one death a month at the full moon. Then two, around the time of the full moon. Now we have two deaths in one night and no moon at all. We seem to have a supernatural serial killer on our hands and no way of stopping him and if word gets out…"

"If word gets out it will be a disaster. For 400 years the Others have managed to live quietly alongside Mortals because humans are happy to believe that they are the summit of life on earth and thus disregard any evidence that there might be challengers for that honour. And the existence of a werewolf may lead to them looking more closely at some other possibilities. Section S is very concerned. Fortunately, I think I may have a plan."

Galbraith raised a doubtful eyebrow.

"I think that the wolf is getting stronger. I don't know how, but something is giving it more power and letting it change more easily. I think that it has set up a lair and it's changing there and hunting locally. If I flood this area with my associates over the next few nights, I think we have a real chance of finding him."

CHAPTER 15: In the werewolf's lair

Garold woke the next morning refreshed and alert. Well, reasonably alert. The Desoxyn had cleared his system quicker than the clonazepam but he still felt a bit muzzy. Staying up after midnight and ripping people's throats out was quite tiring, after all.

He needed to be focussed today. His drink with Marianne had made him realise that political advancement was in his grasp if he played his cards right.

Focus, though, was increasingly difficult to achieve. Lying there with the smell of wolf still hanging in the air of the tiny flat, he wasn't even sure who he was – or, more accurately, *what* he was. Was he Christopher Garold, a Parliamentarian and respected member of the community, who somehow transformed into a wolf-like creature at night and satisfied an unnatural hunger by feeding on the bodies of his victims? Or was he some supernatural creature of the night that was, by an awful twist of fate, doomed to spend its days as a mere mortal, pathetically toadying to the men and women who controlled his future – men and women his night-time self would tear apart without a qualm?

He made himself a cup of coffee and drank it while he watched the morning news on TV. Would there, he wondered, be anything about the killings in Pimlico?

There was. A few seconds about a gang fight. A council refuse worker had been caught up in the violence and killed.

A refuse worker! That had to be wrong, surely. The men he had killed last night were scum: worthless creatures with the smell of the street on them.

The smell! He thought back to the night, struggling with his daytime human brain to remember exactly what his wolf brain had noticed – or not noticed – the night before. There it was, on the second body. Underneath the stink of rubbish a whiff of some sort of industrial cleanser. And, even fainter, a trace of something that might have been aftershave. It was hardly conclusive: even the unemployed shave, but it was not a cheap scent. And, now he came to think of it, the clothes smelt as if they had been laundered not that long ago.

Could it be true? Might he have killed the wrong man?

The headache he had woken up with was getting worse. The tension in his neck and shoulders was spreading and he felt the blood pounding, bringing waves of pain. He really didn't need that right now.

He thought about the crack he had smoked last night: the way it had made him feel. Just a tiny sniff would set him up for the day. After all, he was doing extraordinary things. He was an extraordinary person. Or an extraordinary creature. Whatever.

OK, he had slipped up this time. But it was one man. Did that really matter? Wasn't one death something that could be overlooked in the wider scheme of things?

He deserved the help the drugs could give him. And he could control them. Just as he could control the changes in his body.

Half an hour later, he was on his way to the House. The spring was back in his step: there was a glint in his eye. He was sitting on a committee to look at the problem of rough sleepers. He thought it could be very stimulating.

CHAPTER 16: Old-fashioned police work

Galbraith had taken the afternoon off. It wasn't so much that he felt he needed to catch up on sleep from the night before but rather that he was preparing for the night ahead. He thought it might well be a busy one.

He was right.

The phone rang at half past midnight.

"Two bodies again, but this time they were rough sleepers: under the bridge near Embankment tube. I'll meet you there."

When he arrived the police had already cordoned off the whole area. Pole was waiting for him as he got out of the car.

"The good news is that the police got here very quickly – it's so close to the Houses of Parliament that there's always a lot of police around. The bad news is that it's going to be almost impossible to cover this up, partly for the same reason."

"Did any of your people see anything?"

"We're not sure." He waved his hands in an uncharacteristically hesitant gesture. "After the last couple of killings they were concentrating more around Pimlico, but one of them said he thought he saw something moving west along the river near Vauxhall Bridge. He followed it as far as that little park at the end of St George's Square but then he lost it. He did say there was a distinctive odour where it had passed. We're getting a dog team in."

The two detectives made their way under the railway bridge where a white forensic tent marked the spot where the first body lay. Pole went in to look at the body while Galbraith just lifted the flap back for a moment to confirm that it was similar to the previous attacks. Pole emerged a few minutes later.

"Same MO," he said. "Even more vicious than before if that's possible. Let's have a look at the other one."

A little further back under the bridge there is a small road with a parade of shops where the business of retail is continually interrupted by the noise of the trains going overhead. It's a quiet location (apart from the trains) and after the shops shut up for the night it is often used for shelter by those with nowhere else to sleep. About halfway down, another white tent marked the werewolf's latest kill.

Again Pole spent a few minutes in the tent while Galbraith loitered outside, pretending an interest in the crime scene.

Emerging, Pole looked grim. “There’s no doubt it’s him. But these are definitely street people. It’s a change from his other victims.”

“And a change of location.”

Pole shook his head. “I’m not sure about that. If I’m right and he’s set up some sort of lair, it could well be about halfway between here and the Abbots Estate. He’s come out of his front door and turned left instead of right. It fits the idea of something being seen in the general direction of St George’s Square – on its way back from killing, presumably.” He sniffed the night air. “Let's go and see how the dog teams are getting on. The walk will do us good."

* * *

It’s a half hour walk from Hungerford Bridge to St George’s Square and Pole set off at his usual rapid pace. Galbraith found he was short of breath as he tried to match Pole’s stride, but he panted out his question anyway.

“How are you planning to explain these deaths?"

“It might be simplest to say that the dog reported on the Winstanley Estate has apparently moved into town. People should be on their guard. Police will be going door to door in an attempt to gather information that might track it down.”

“Will we?”

Pole slowed for a moment. “I think we might very well. Let’s see what the dogs have found.”

By the time they had reached St George’s Square, Galbraith was breathing hard. Pole looked at him with concern. “You aren’t getting any younger, you know. My offer is still open. Admittedly I’m not getting any younger either, but were you to transfer to Section S full-time, as it were, you wouldn’t get any older.” He smiled. “More time to work on your tango.”

“Perhaps not.”

He had automatically used the conventionally polite phrase, but as he said it, he realised that the word ‘perhaps’ had slipped out. One of his Shakespearian references seemed appropriate: ‘Many a true word hath been spoken in jest.’ Or was the better quote something to do with Freud?

There was one of the plain dark vans that Galbraith associated with Section S parked at the river end of St George's Square and some very big dogs – about the size of Irish wolfhounds – were sniffing enthusiastically at the ground nearby.

"Unusual dogs," remarked Galbraith. "What are they?"

"They're a sort of bloodhound."

"Really? They look rather large for bloodhounds."

"Yes," said Pole. "They're bred specially."

"Specially for what?"

"Oh, you know." Pole was trying to sound airily dismissive but, in Galbraith's view, noticeably failing. "Times when you might want to be tracking a creature on the large side."

Galbraith gave a quizzical look and waited for more but Pole developed a sudden interest in the view down to the river and Galbraith realised that he was not going to find out what quarry the dogs had been trained to hunt. He decided he would probably sleep better for not knowing.

Pole had now turned his attention back to the dogs and their handlers.

"Anything?" he asked.

"There was something. It's vanished into this greenery and we can't see where it's come out."

Galbraith looked at the greenery. It was the sort of open space that you often found in the centre of London squares – mainly grass, much of it trampled to mud at this time of year, and a few bushes and trees dotted here and there. There didn't really seem any space for a wolf to hide.

"Perhaps it changed back to human form in the square?"

Pole shook his head. "Unlikely. Even if the process has been speeded up somehow, it's hardly instantaneous and it's vulnerable when it's changing. It's going to want to take shelter somewhere. Think of the changing hut on Clapham Common. I think he has somewhere near here. And that's where house-to-house comes in."

"What, knocking on doors and asking if you know any werewolves?"

"Knocking on doors and saying that we are worried about the killer dog they will have read about in the newspapers. Do they have any outbuildings or sheds that it could be in? Have they seen anything suspicious? Were they around last night? And we ask your policemen to make a discreet note of anybody that they talk to who is slim build, brown haired, and about 6 feet tall. And ask if there is anybody else in the house. I doubt that our werewolf is sharing his accommodation.

We're looking for people who meet that description, live alone in the area and were home at least some of last night."

"It's a bit of a long shot, isn't it?"

"Most of Sherlock Holmes' reasoning involved far more long shots than that, but he's still held up as the great detective."

"Sherlock Holmes is a work of fiction."

"Not entirely. Mr Conan Doyle and I enjoyed many chats about police work. He incorporated some of my experiences into his stories. For example, you were remarking on our tracker dogs. Have you ever read 'The Hound of the Baskervilles'?"

Galbraith could think of no sensible reply to that, so he said nothing.

"Excellent," said Pole. "I suggest you get back to the station in time to get the house-to-house started first thing before people leave for work."

Galbraith looked at his watch. If he made it home quickly, he might well manage four hours' sleep. He thought of Shakespeare's views on sleep: 'Sleep that knits up the ravell'd sleave of care.' Galbraith believed that you could guide your life by what Shakespeare had written. When this was all over, he promised himself, he was going to make a serious effort to spend more time in bed.

* * *

At 7.00am Galbraith was in Belgravia police station briefing the early shift on the house-to-house. He suspected that many of the men and women on parade were not that impressed with the idea that they were concentrating their attention on a search for a dangerous dog rather than any of the apparently more serious crimes in the area. Galbraith reminded them that it had killed three people already and they looked appropriately serious as they recorded the details of his orders in their notebooks. There were some puzzled frowns at the request to look out for tall, slim brown-haired men, but these details were duly written down too.

Back in his own office, Galbraith started on a report on rough sleepers around Earls Court. Superintendent Bailey had asked for it. "There's some Parliamentary committee talking about it so the top brass want us to have our ducks in a row for when the MPs decide it's all our problem." Galbraith had smiled politely and agreed to get on with it. It made a change from CCTV and gave him something to do while he waited for the results from the house-to-house. The early shift comes off duty at three, so he expected to get the first reports soon after.

In the event he had to wait until almost 4.00, but the delay was worth it. Somebody in Belgravia had consolidated all the results into a very short list of men living alone in that area who fitted the description.

Galbraith read the list and was straight on his way to Pole's apartment.

Pole claimed not to own a phone – clearly nonsense as he had proved by waking Galbraith with his calls whenever the werewolf struck. Galbraith suspected it was one of the ways in which Pole took a stand against the 21st century. He functioned well enough in the modern world but often gave the impression that he might have been happier living in the past. Pole's explanation was that the apartment was his home, rather than his office – but he had yet to admit to ever being in an office other than Galbraith's. He also explained that he was sleeping during the day so wasn't around to take phone calls anyway. Galbraith wondered if another reason was that it enhanced the mystique of the secretive section that he worked for. Not that it worried him much. If he needed to talk to Pole he would rather do it face to face and his apartment was a much nicer place than Galbraith's office.

Pole had also been waiting for the information gathered in the house-to-house enquiries. Galbraith was fairly certain, though that he hadn't spent the time writing a report on rough sleepers.

He passed the list to Pole and waited while he read through it.

"Six possibles," said Pole. "That's a start at any rate."

"Better than that." Galbraith allowed a trace of smugness into his voice. It wasn't often that he was ahead of Pole and he allowed himself to enjoy the moment. "We were wondering why our canine friend had suddenly switched to rough sleepers. I think I might know the answer."

Pole raised an interrogative eyebrow.

"Yesterday there was a Parliamentary committee discussing rough sleepers and this name…" Galbraith stabbed a finger at the list. "… is an MP."

Pole's lips twitched into a smile. "Tall, slim, brown hair?"

"Lives alone, home last night. And would you like to guess where he is MP for?"

"Christopher Garold, MP for Richmond East. I should have seen it earlier."

"I don't think we can blame ourselves for that. But it does explain a lot."

"Indeed it does. Do we know where he is now?"

"Not for sure, but the House of Commons seems a reasonable bet."

Pole twitched aside one of the curtains that were always drawn firmly closed. "I do like these months: practically dark by four o'clock. I think it would be a nice evening for a walk."

Parliament, Galbraith reckoned, was more than a half-hour walk from Pole's apartment. He really didn't want another of Pole's forced marches through the evening traffic.

"Given how often he's attacking, we need to move as quickly as we can. Perhaps we should take a taxi."

To his surprise, Pole didn't argue.

"That's a good idea. I need to carry something with me and a taxi might be convenient."

He vanished into the corridor that led from the study into the interior of the flat and rooms that Galbraith had never been invited into. He returned with a leather gladstone bag that had a patina that suggested it was old enough that it might once have belonged to Gladstone himself. Pole set it down on the floor and something inside it rattled metallically.

"Right," he said. "Let's be on our way."

CHAPTER 17: In which Garold has a good lunch and a bad afternoon

Garold couldn't remember the last time he had felt as good as this. The killings of the night before had left him feeling somehow cleansed and he had slept better than he remembered in years.

He didn't even need the crack cocaine to sharpen him ready for the day ahead, but he allowed himself a sniff anyway. He deserved it.

It hardly seemed worth spending another afternoon discussing homeless vagrants on the committee room corridor. His efforts last night had, he felt, done more to tackle the problem of rough sleepers than all the talk in Parliament in the past year. Tonight he would clear some more of the garbage off the streets.

Then he remembered his talk with Marianne. He would turn up. He would say all the right things in the committee. The word would go to the Prime Minister. Garold was sound. Garold could be relied on. Garold was a man who would fit very well in government.

He dressed carefully – even more carefully than usual. College tie, to appeal to the traditionalists; Armani suit to identify with the younger men on the way up, patterned socks to show he was an individualist. The old Greenpeace sweatshirt and cargo pants were reserved for seeing environmental activists at the weekends – and if he was made a minister, he could reasonably claim that there were too many pressures on his time for him to be able to keep on meeting them.

He enjoyed the walk to the House. It was a beautiful morning and the air from the river went some way to diluting the traffic fumes along Millbank.

He dodged through the traffic on Bridge Street and entered Portcullis House at a half-run, shouting a cheery “Good morning!” to the security guard as he passed. Today, he was sure, was going to be a good day.

Even the pile of correspondence waiting on his office desk would not depress him. He employed a part-time secretary – a middle aged lady of impeccable rectitude who came in three mornings a week to deal with his post. He had made a positive decision not to have the full-time assistants and interns that most MPs employed because he liked the feeling that he was a free spirit, untrammelled by the bureaucracy that ended up crushing so many of his colleagues. He thought again about his conversation with the whip. (In truth, he had thought about it almost every waking hour since it had happened – at least while he was in human form.) If he was to find a job in government, he would probably need to have more help in the office.

He favoured the woman with a particularly enthusiastic smile. “Morning, Beatrice, am I late?”

“Not at all, Mr Garold. I was a little early.”

He liked the ‘Mr Garold.’ He thought it was good to be informal in public but here, in his office, he preferred the old-fashioned courtesies.

“Let’s get cracking then, shall we?”

Nowadays, most of his constituency casework was dealt with by his constituency office where a younger assistant and an intern dealt with the problems of the voters of Richmond East – though they were always careful to make sure he got the credit for any problems solved. The letters that he had to deal with himself were those from lobbyists – both amateur (like the local Greenpeace members) and professional (like the PR company acting for a major oil producer) – and those that his assistant decided needed his personal touch. He took his job seriously and gave all of them his attention. Unlike some of his colleagues, he did not allow himself to be influenced by the fact that the oil company was offering a fact-finding tour in the Gulf of Mexico while Greenpeace was inviting him to attend the meeting in Roehampton on a Saturday afternoon. He did allow himself to spend more time on a constituency problem that might make the local press than on an issue that would arouse no interest outside the immediate circle of the aggrieved constituent, but he was, after all, only human (most of the time). He made an honest effort with all of his post and Beatrice was kept busy with her shorthand pad while he dealt with one letter after another, sometimes calling a council official or a government office to put his personal weight behind a constituent’s complaint. He had always seen it as his duty to serve his constituents and he did so conscientiously, even if much of the routine stuff never got beyond his constituency office. He employed the staff there and the job got done – which he felt fulfilled his side of an MP’s bargain with the voters.

Today his eyes were that bit brighter and his responses that bit faster. His drug enhanced morning regime, he thought, was making him an even more efficient public servant. His constituents should be delighted.

Besides the letters from constituents and the circulars with briefing notes that the party sent to all its MPs, there was one message that stood out. Sir Digby Monroe would like to meet him for lunch.

Not many people would expect Garold to drop any other plans he might have in order to make a lunch appointment at only a few hours' notice. But Sir Digby Monroe was different. He was the Prime Minister's closest adviser. The PM made no significant decisions that weren't run past Sir Digby first – and that would include new appointments to government.

Garold finished the last of his correspondence, thanked Beatrice and sent her on her way. Her immaculately typed replies would spew out of his printer that afternoon in plenty of time for him to sign them and put them in the post tray before the last Portcullis House collection. Some MPs, he knew, resorted to emails, sparing themselves a few minutes of signing letters and putting them in envelopes. (Once he was a minister, he realised, Beatrice could stay all day and deal with the tedious mechanics of the post.) Garold recognised the value that constituents put on the heavy paper with the green House of Commons letterhead. A few minutes more dealing with his post was surely worthwhile for the goodwill it generated.

For now his correspondence was in Beatrice's safe hands and he was left with half an hour to visit the washrooms and make sure that his appearance was immaculate before his lunch appointment. There had been some unfortunate press photographs of government ministers looking as if they had just rolled out of a bar (often because they had) and the PM was said to be insisting that looking the part was a prerequisite for future candidates for office.

His hair was impeccably cut and neatly combed. He had worried that the constant switching between his normal hair and the coarse dark pelt of the wolf might have left him looking the worse for wear, but the image in the mirror reassured him. The eyes looked a little dull after the slightly manic brightness of that morning, but, in the absence of another crack hit, he was sure that a lunchtime drink would perk him up.

He was carefully prompt to the Members' Dining Room. Sir Digby, he was assured, had made a reservation but not yet arrived. Perhaps he would like to have a drink while he waited. Yes, he thought he would.

He ordered a G&T. It was a little stronger than he would normally drink at lunchtime, but he needed something to revive the buzz of the early morning.

He had a vague memory of talking to a youth worker in Richmond who was explaining that, while there were few heroin addicts in leafy West London, there were problems with uppers and downers. "It's when they take the two together that you get real problems. They interact and the results can be unpredictable, especially when alcohol is involved." Or had he said that alcohol reduced uptake of the drugs? That seemed reasonable. Perhaps he should have another G&T.

Before he could catch a waiter's eye to give his order, Sir Digby strode in. "Sorry I'm late," he said. "Meeting with the PM ran over."

Sir Digby, Garold thought, had never been subtle when it came to broadcasting his own importance.

"Please don't apologise. I've only just arrived."

The empty glass rather gave the lie to this, but Sir Digby was already summoning a waiter with the menu. "Steak," he said, hardly glancing at it. "Rare. With French fries and whatever is your veg of the day." He looked at Garold. "What are you having?"

Garold, who had barely had time to open the menu, decided to go with the same. In the past he preferred his steak well done, but his nocturnal expeditions had left him with a taste for meat that was distinctly on the raw side.

"Wise choice," said Sir Digby. "You can't go wrong with a rare steak. And I thought Malbec."

A Malbec, Garold assured him would be fine.

The meal, Garold felt, went well – very well. He sparkled. He was witty and intelligent and well-informed, talking confidently about government policy and the strengths and weaknesses of the PM. The Malbec had slid down well and he had ordered a second bottle, insisting that this should be put on his account. He knew better than to try to slip it on Sir Digby's bill. The PM's adviser had nodded apparent approval, though he had waved away the waiter who tried to top up his glass. He was in a hurry, Garold realised and, indeed, soon after that, he left, explaining that he had a meeting with the Chief Whip. It had gone well, though, Garold thought and he was confident that Sir Digby would throw his weight behind any suggestion that Garold be given a government job.

The afternoon was another session of the committee discussing homelessness in London and, with promotion in the offing, Garold was careful to be in his seat early. He did not speak during the session. In the past he might have made an effort to get a useful soundbite in, but with promotions so close he couldn't do anything to advance his cause and an injudicious remark might damage him. In fact, once or twice he dozed off – it had been a very good lunch – but he was not the only MP to catch up on sleep on the committee room corridor and, provided you didn't snore, it was not usually held against you.

The session had been scheduled to run until around 5.30, but soon after 4.00 phones began pinging and the air of lethargy in the room suddenly lifted. Garold felt the nervous excitement of his Conservative colleagues and realised that news of the long-awaited reshuffle was coming through.

He looked at his own phone. His WhatsApp feed was scrolling updates on who was in and who was out, but there were no messages for him.

The Chair brought the meeting to an early end. Nothing was going to get done while MPs compared notes and rushed off to ingratiate themselves with those on the up and to commiserate (or gloat) with those who had fallen from office.

Garold wasn't worried. There would be a message in time. But perhaps he should check in with Marianne, just in case there had been some kind of glitch. Phones had been known to fail. Emails were sometimes lost in hyperspace.

He made his way along the long corridor and into the warren of offices that led off the west end of it. This was where the whips had their lair.

Marianne was in her office but as soon as he appeared in the doorway she gave a distinct impression that she would rather be somewhere else. Seeing the expression on her face, Garold wondered, for the first time, if something might have gone terribly wrong. Not that anyone would have thought so from the confident smile on his face.

"Hi, Marianne. I was wondering if you knew what was going on."

She gave a tight smile, very unlike the welcoming beam that she had favoured him with only the day before. "I hope I know what's going on, Christopher. It's pretty much the definition of my job."

"And a couple of days ago your job seems to have included a broad hint that I could expect to hear good news in the reshuffle."

"Indeed. But we all make mistakes, Christopher. It is not for us to know every detail of the PM's mind."

Garold sank down into the chair opposite the whip's desk.

"What happened?" His voice was hoarse.

"You blew it, Christopher. You were a bloody idiot and you blew it. The PM wanted you, everyone agreed you were solid, and then Sir Digby asked if he could look you over. It was a formality – a quick lunch and you were in. That's why it was so last minute. Nobody thought it was anything but rubber stamping the new job. And you blew it."

She looked at him as if he were a bad smell.

"Do you want to know what he said about you?"

There was a sheet of paper on the desk and she picked it up and read from it. "Arrogant. Cocksure. Rude. Apparently drunk. Do you want me to go on?"

Garold sat, stunned. Marianne seemed to take his silence as a 'yes'.

"Immature, irritating, totally unsuitable for serious office. And that's without the personally offensive bits."

He could feel the anger rising now. He could, he thought, actually feel the blood coursing through his veins and the cocktail of drugs and alcohol swirling through his body. And something else: something that should only be glimpsed in darkness.

He opened his mouth to speak and what came out was a howl of rage. An animal howl that had Marianne shrink back in her chair, her face pale. She began to scream. For such a small woman, she screamed very loudly.

He had to get out of there! He threw open the door and plunged into the corridor, turning right and left, unsure now where he was until he emerged onto the committee corridor, stretching straight and empty ahead of him.

CHAPTER 18: Unparliamentary behaviour

Galbraith had spent the taxi ride trying to find out where Christopher Garold was likely to be. He rang his office, where Beatrice had left to type up his letters from her home. His constituency office did answer the phone but only to say that Mr Garold was in the House and would get in touch as soon as he was free. He even tried the Parliamentary Security Department, which works with the Metropolitan police to provide security at Westminster. He was kept on hold for five minutes while they confirmed that he was, in fact, a policeman, only to be told that they had no idea where Garold was. "Your best bet is to ask the Whips' Office," they said. "It's their job to know where MPs are. Our job is just to make sure they don't get killed while they're doing whatever it is they do."

The taxi pulled up by the gates of parliament and Pole used his warrant card and a parliamentary pass to whisk them by security.

"You have a pass?" Galbraith asked.

"Of course. I've been coming here a long time."

They hurried through the great doorway of Westminster Hall, their footsteps echoing on the stone floor. It was eerily empty but Pole headed confidently up the steps opposite the entrance and turned sharply left down a short corridor into the grand central lobby. After the emptiness of Westminster Hall, the lobby seemed filled with people but Pole headed straight through as if they weren't there. Galbraith watched MPs, used to deference from visitors, move automatically out of his way without even realising they were doing so. Pole could have that effect on people. "Best way to the whips is down the committee corridor." He hurried straight on, down another passageway and a smaller hall and then up a flight of stairs, almost running as they passed the busts of dead prime ministers lined against the walls like some macabre guard of honour. They emerged from the staircase onto a long, windowless passage. "The Committee Corridor," announced Pole. "We turn left."

As they turned, they heard screaming from somewhere beyond the far end of the corridor. They began to run towards the sound just as they saw a figure appear around the corner. It was a fair way off – the corridor seemed ridiculously long – but it was clear, even at that distance, that there was something wrong about it.

It looked like a man, but the way that it walked was not entirely human. It seemed to be stumbling and, as they watched, it started to wave its arms, as if writhing in pain. But still it stumbled towards them and they ran towards it. They could see it more clearly now. It was wearing a suit. Galbraith knew little about bespoke tailoring but, even to him, even at a distance, this was plainly an expensive suit – but it didn't seem to fit properly. Even as he watched, the man – or what still looked like a man – waved his arms again and there was tearing sound and the seam opened on the shoulder.

There was another figure in the corridor now. Another man – tall, thin, slightly gangly – was hurrying after the first. This man, though, was very definitely human. "For fuck's sake, Garold! Stop running!" There was something uncomfortably hilarious about the obscenity being shouted in an accent that had clearly been formed in a very exclusive school. Galbraith, though, did not see the humour in it.

"Christopher Garold!" he shouted. "You're under arrest."

Garold ignored him and kept on moving forwards. The shambling gait was changing into a run. There was another tearing sound from the suit as the legs seemed to lengthen.

The creature was coming at him fast now. Galbraith didn't think of it as a man anymore. The face was covered in hair and as Galbraith watched the shape seemed to be changing. It opened its mouth and Galbraith saw teeth that were definitely not human.

He remembered what Pole had said – that the creature was at his weakest as it changed form. Instead of ducking aside, Galbraith dropped his shoulder and charged forward, barrelling into its chest.

It was like throwing himself into an oncoming locomotive and about as effective. Galbraith was swept aside, crashing onto the carpet.

Only now did the creature stop, turning to look down at him. It opened its jaws and Galbraith felt its saliva dripping onto his face. He twisted his head away and saw Pole, who was still holding his ridiculous bag and struggling to run, drop the bag to the ground. He bent down to it and came out holding a gun. Not any gun, but one that even Garold could recognise as an old Colt six-shooter. Wherever it had come from, Pole had definitely not had it issued by a Metropolitan Police armoury.

Regulations say that police officers are supposed to shout, "Armed police!" before opening fire. Pole wasted no time on such niceties. He raised the gun and pulled the trigger.

A Colt Single Action Army revolver is a big gun and the sound of the shot echoed around the corridor. Galbraith's ears were ringing and time slowed as Garold – or the thing that had been Garold – staggered back, blood pouring from a wound in its shoulder.

The smoke from the barrel of the Colt started to clear and time seemed to pass faster. Galbraith rolled the creature onto its stomach and pulled its arms behind it, snapping on handcuffs and ratcheting them tight.

As its wounded shoulder was jerked backwards, the creature howled in pain. Galbraith watched in horror as it pulled against the handcuffs and the hardened steel shattered.

Before it could get to his feet, Pole was on it. He had pulled a set of manacles from the bag. They looked to Galbraith like something out of a museum, but Pole closed them on Garold's arms and screwed them shut.

Galbraith watched in disbelief. Garold had just broken open the latest that the 21st century had to offer in the way of restraints. What on earth made Pole think that these ancient shackles would hold? Yet, though Garold threshed and pulled against them, they held.

"Iron," Pole explained. "Iron is good against all manner of magical creatures. Present company excluded, of course."

The tall man had arrived to join them, slightly out of breath and clearly shocked by what he had just seen, but he immediately took charge of the situation. He opened the nearest door. "Get him in here," he ordered. He had the natural authority of those who had generations of command in their blood. Almost without conscious thought, Galbraith and Pole half dragged, half carried Garold through the door.

"Best keep him out of sight."

Now that the adrenalin from the attack was subsiding Galbraith asked the question he realised he should have asked earlier.

"Who the hell are you?"

"Thomas Robson." He offered his hand and Galbraith shook it automatically. "Chief Whip. I'm afraid this fellow is my responsibility."

"Not any longer," said Galbraith. "This is very much a police matter. He's under arrest."

Robson looked pained. “I’m embarrassed to have to mention it, but I’m afraid you may be exceeding your authority there.”

“We have evidence he has killed several times. As far as I’m concerned, he’s nicked.”

“I’m terribly sorry,” — and Galbraith thought he did look genuinely apologetic – "but you can’t arrest an MP in the precincts of the House.”

“Oh, come on! That’s just a technical thing. I go to the sergeant whatsit…”

“The Serjeant at Arms,” Robson said, helpfully.

“Him. I go to him and he hands the fellow over to me.”

“Not if the Government asks him not to.”

“And why the hell would they do that?”

“Because it’s not in anybody’s interest to say that there has been a supernatural creature…” He looked at the shackled body. The bleeding had already stopped and the wound appeared to be healing. “You should have used a silver bullet.” He looked at Pole. “It is what I think it is, isn't it?”

“Yes, it is a werewolf and no, I should not have used a silver bullet because I didn’t want to kill it.”

The Chief Whip raised an eyebrow.

“It can’t help being a werewolf. If we start executing non-humans on sight for being what they are, it could have unfortunate consequences. These things can get out of hand very quickly.”

“I take it you have a personal interest in this matter.”

Galbraith felt it was time to stop whatever it was that was going on with these two. He was already dealing with a vampire and a werewolf and he was beginning to have his doubts about the Chief Whip. He felt Pole was absolutely correct when he said that these things can get out of hand very quickly. “Can we concentrate on the fact that I have a suspect in custody and I would like to see him taken to a police station and charged?”

He looked down at his prisoner. The man was a mess: suit torn, shoes missing, hair unkempt and what looked like the world’s heaviest five o’clock shadow, but it was now definitely a man. “This is Christopher Garold. I don’t have to mention werewolves.”

“And if you don’t,” said Robson, “what will you charge him with?"

"Yes," said Pole. "That’s a bit of a quandary, isn’t it?”

They all looked down at the figure on the floor. It was now fully human and clearly Christopher Garold, albeit a very dishevelled Christopher Garold.

"It seems a fair question," said Garold.

Galbraith looked from werewolf to vampire to – well, whatever Robson was. He felt that he had rather lost control of the situation.

"Are you suggesting I just let him go?"

"Of course not." Robson was soothingly urbane. "Hand him over to me. I'll take care of him."

Galbraith was still trying to take in what Robson was suggesting when Pole said, "Can we trust you?"

"Do you really have a choice?"

When Pole did not reply, Robson went on: "You can't charge him as a human. You can't admit he's a werewolf without creating panic and searches for other supernatural creatures. Mr Pole, quite properly, will object to your shooting him out of hand. I agree that he can't simply be turned out onto the streets where he might kill again. So I remain your last best hope. The Palace of Westminster is large and full of mysterious passages that are very seldom visited. It's famously easy to get lost in. There are rooms in the cellars that I'm happy to accept have not been opened for decades. Mr Garold can remain within the Palace indefinitely. By day, he will go about his business as an MP and at night he can sleep in an apartment I will arrange for him. And at full moon that apartment will be kept locked, just to be on the safe side."

"Can you really do that?" asked Galbraith.

"My dear boy," said Robson, "I'm the Chief Whip. I can do anything. It's practically my job description."

"And if it goes wrong and he gets out?"

"As soon as he leaves the Palace of Westminster, you are free to arrest him."

"That still leaves the question of what we can arrest him for."

Robson gave a thin-lipped smile. "I think that if you were to search his home, you would find enough class A drugs to form the basis of a charge."

Garold, who was by now sitting up and following the conversation, turned pale. "How could you possibly know that?"

"I'm the Chief Whip," said Robson. "I know everything."

Pole grinned.

Galbraith found that disconcerting. He had never seen Pole grin before.

“I think,” Pole said, “that now would be a very good time for us to leave.” He turned to Robson. “You can keep the shackles. You never know: they might come in useful.”

He took Galbraith’s arm and steered him towards the door.

Galbraith was too stunned to resist.

* * *

Pole steered Galbraith into an empty office. “You look a bit shaken, which is understandable. Deep breaths and sit tight. I need a word with Mr Robson,” he had said. “And I need to make a few calls.”

Galbraith hadn’t argued. He wasn’t sure whether the shock from being attacked by a werewolf was more stunning that the conversation with the Chief Whip or the other way round, but the two between them had left him struggling to cope.

When Pole returned, he led him out onto Abingdon Street and hailed a taxi. Clearly, he did not think Galbraith was up to walking anywhere. They drove straight to Pole’s apartment where he had wasted no time in getting Galbraith settled in an armchair with a larger than usual glass of whisky.

“What just happened?”

“An awkward situation was dealt with,” said Pole.

“You’ll struggle to cover that one up.”

“Not really. Thanks to the reshuffle, the Committee Corridor was practically deserted. We’re going to explain that the killer dog we have been looking for was a wolf that had escaped from somewhere. Sadly, we don’t know where. It somehow got into the Houses of Parliament where it was shot dead by armed police.”

“Won’t people want to see the wolf?”

“Indeed. Which is why Section S has made a substantial donation to the Zoological Society of London. Even now a heavily tranquilised wolf has been transferred from Whipsnade and put on display to press photographers at the very spot where it was shot. Stage blood will feature. It will be very convincing.”

“And the marksman?”

“Cannot be identified for security reasons.”

"There must have been some witnesses. I heard screams."

"People construct their memories. They can't have seen a werewolf – that would be ridiculous – so they don't remember seeing the werewolf. An actual escaped wolf is odd but there's the evidence of the photograph and the press release, so that's what they will remember having seen."

"Which just leaves the future life of Christopher Garold and his Chief Whip. There was something very peculiar about Mr Robson and I can't help thinking that you knew more about him that you were letting on. He's not one of yours, is he?"

"Good heavens, no. He is as human as you are. More or less. He's a Mage."

"A Mage?"

"A wizard, if you prefer. He has been studying magic all his life – and he's considerably older than he looks."

Galbraith frowned. "But he's an MP."

"Not just an MP: he's the Chief Whip. It's not a high-profile job, but it exercises real power. It's exactly the sort of job a Mage would hold."

"But what will he do with Garold?"

Pole poured himself another whisky and sat back in his chair. "I really have no idea. But Garold is his problem now. As far as Section S is concerned, this is very definitely 'Case Closed.'"

CHAPTER 19: In which Garold finds a new life

Thomas Robson had arranged for Christopher Garold's clothes to be collected from St George's Square and transferred to his new home in the Palace of Westminster. When the Chief Whip made his way down into the corridors below the Chamber, Garold was looking his normal suave self.

"Any problems from the wound?"

Garold moved his shoulder experimentally. "It seems to have healed remarkably well."

"That's one of the benefits of your condition." Robson looked around the room. "You should be comfortable here. You're very privileged. There's just you and the Speaker with your own apartments in the Palace. Convenient for your office, too."

"So you're expecting me to stay on as an MP." Garold had to admit he was surprised. He had thought that being a shape-shifting supernatural being was a disqualification from office.

"Not just staying on, dear boy. You're being promoted."

For a moment Garold wondered if the drugs were still in his system. Then, looking at the amused expression on Robson's face, he grew so angry that, for a moment, he feared that he might begin to change again. "Mocking me is beneath you, Robson. Marianne told me I was in line for promotion and I threw that away. There's no need to rub it in."

"You're right. You were due for promotion and you, as you put it, threw it away. You were going to be roads minister."

Robson's amusement was obvious. Making one of the few sincere environmentalists in the party responsible for the road building programme was positively Machiavellian.

"That was your idea, wasn't it?"

"It was indeed. With a majority as slim as ours we need the young radicals like you carefully bottled up in a safe place." He looked around at the elegantly appointed, notably windowless, room where they were sitting. "The political equivalent of this in a way, I suppose."

"So what are you talking about now?"

"I want you to join the Whips' Office."

"Are you serious?"

"Completely. Given your circumstances, you are in no position to make trouble for the Government. Making trouble for them means making trouble for me and you exist at my discretion. It seemed to me that Chief Inspector Galbraith would be only too happy to take you off my hands if you are a nuisance. So you are loyal. But not all your colleagues are as loyal as you will be. Now, as you know, we whips have our ways of persuading people to do as they are told."

Garold did, indeed, know. It was believed that the whips kept files on all their MPs detailing their sexual peccadilloes, their financial irregularities – even the telephone numbers of their drug dealers. When votes were tight, things could get very nasty.

"Strangely, though," Robson continued, "we have some MPs so upstanding that we really have nothing that we can use to persuade them. And others so debauched that there is nothing left to threaten them with. Now some Chief Whips have dealt with such people by having some large and threatening colleagues whose mere physical presence encourages recalcitrant MPs to toe the line. Such people are sometimes referred to as 'attack dogs'. Do you see where I am going with this?"

Garold thought he could see all too clearly.

"We don't want any actual violence," said Robson. "Just the occasional reminder that I like to run a tight ship."

"So I behave myself and can spend the rest of my life locked away in here?"

"We'll arrange for you to visit your constituency from time to time, with appropriate supervision, of course." Robson placed a reassuring hand on Garold's shoulder. "It's not a bad life. And you will get out on your own occasionally."

"Really?"

"Absolutely. When I feel it would be a good idea."

CHAPTER 20: Case closed

With the case officially closed, Galbraith expected that he wouldn't see Pole again for a while, if ever, but the vampire made a definite effort to stay in touch.

"You've been very useful to Section S," he said. "We wouldn't want to lose you. I'm simply trying to keep you in the loop if there are any interesting developments in our area of work." But when they met, invariably at his flat, there was no conversation about Section S's activities at all. Pole would ask about the regular police work that Galbraith was involved in and would make occasional suggestions about likely culprits – suggestions that almost always led to an arrest. Mostly, though, they sat quietly, sipping their whisky. Sometimes Pole would put on tango music and Galbraith would be transported back to the first case they had worked on together and he would promise himself that he would make more effort to learn the dance. Pole seemed to know what was in his mind and would smile as they sat together listening. It was almost as though, Galbraith thought, they had become friends.

One evening, though, Galbraith arrived carrying a newspaper. He opened it at a story about a journalist who had apparently been savaged by a dog in Camden.

"No witnesses," said Galbraith, "just a very large dog which suddenly turns up in Camden, takes a chunk out of this fellow's arm and then vanishes away."

Pole's face was unreadable.

Galbraith waved the newspaper at him."

"It was a full moon last night."

Pole took the paper and glanced at the article.

"Don't pretend you know nothing about it," said Galbraith. "It's exactly the sort of thing Section S is there to deal with."

"It says here that the man suffered a nasty bite but no more than that. Nobody died. There's nothing there to interest Section S."

Galbraith had conducted a lot of interrogations in his lifetime. He knew when the best way to get someone to open up was to say nothing at all.

Eventually Pole broke an increasingly uncomfortable silence.

"What would you have me do? Order his death?"

"Could you?"

"It might be possible. Thomas Robson is a powerful man. There might be consequences. But Section S could probably handle it."

"Then why not?"

"Garold is Robson's creature now. If he was responsible for the injuries to that journalist, shouldn't we be taking action against Robson? Garold did not kill. He controls his urges, as I do."

"You care about him."

"Of course I do. I told you that we Others are just that – Others. And we have been alone for so long. It is good to know that we are a little less alone than we were."

Galbraith rose from his seat and poured Pole another drink. He felt the vampire needed it.

"You're not completely alone, even now," he said.

Pole smiled. "My offer still stands," he said.

"One day, maybe," said Galbraith. "Until then, remember that there is at least one human happy to keep company with you."

They sipped their drinks. The silence now was companionable and lasted a long time.

Eventually Galbraith finished his drink and stood.

"I need to be getting home. Until tomorrow?"

"Yes," said Pole. "Until tomorrow."

* * *

The last tube had gone. Galbraith decided to walk for a while. He made his way along the river. There was still traffic, of course, but it seemed peaceful, even, occasionally, quiet. Overhead, the moon was almost full, clearly visible, even against the lights of London. He caught himself looking over his shoulder. Without conscious thought, he began walking faster.

Somewhere in the distance he imagined that he could hear the howling of a wolf.

A NOTE FROM ME

This book is my third contemporary fantasy. Usually I write historical novels, but I'm really enjoyed the change of pace and style these books bring.

This is the second book to feature Galbraith and Pole. The first, *Something Wicked* is available on Amazon.

As always, I have to thank the people who have helped by reading and commenting on early drafts: Paul Benedyk, Jennifer Macaire, John Haines, Ruben Aszkenasy and Stan Barker. Special thanks are due to my family, and especially my wife, Tammy, who put up with a lot.

Details of my other books are all on my website: tomwilliamsauthor.co.uk. There are regular blog posts there too, ranging over everything from Napoleon's life on Elba to the etiquette of asking for a dance in a Buenos Aires tango bar. If you have enjoyed reading this story, you might enjoy some of my writing there. (You can write to me through the site too.)

For all but a few famous authors whose books you will see widely advertised, the only way to get our books read is by word-of-mouth. If you have enjoyed the book, please tell your friends. Better yet, if you have a couple of minutes to spare it will make a huge difference if you could say something about it on Amazon – just a few words will do.

Thank you.

OTHER BOOKS BY TOM WILLIAMS

James Burke, spy

Burke in the Land of Silver

Burke and the Bedouin

Burke at Waterloo

Burke in the Peninsula

Burke in Ireland

Burke and the Pimpernel Affair

The Williamson Papers
(Adventures in the age of Empire)

The White Rajah

Cawnpore

Back Home

Contemporary Urban Fantasy

Dark Magic

Something Wicked